WITHDRAWN

Final Fall

Also by Heather W. Petty

Lock & Mori
Mind Games

LOCK &MORI

FINAL FALL

HEATHER W. PETTY

SIMON & SCHUSTER BFYR

New York   London   Toronto   Sydney   New Delhi

SIMON & SCHUSTER BFYR

An imprint of Simon & Schuster Children's Publishing Division
1230 Avenue of the Americas, New York, New York 10020

SIMON & SCHUSTER BFYR is a trademark of Simon & Schuster, Inc.
For information about special discounts for bulk purchases, please contact Simon & Schuster Special Sales at 1-866-506-1949 or business@simonandschuster.com.
The Simon & Schuster Speakers Bureau can bring authors to your live event. For more information or to book an event, contact the Simon & Schuster Speakers Bureau at 1-866-248-3049 or visit our website at www.simonspeakers.com.
Book design by Krista Vossen
The text for this book was set in Bembo Std.
Manufactured in the United States of America
First Edition
10 9 8 7 6 5 4 3 2 1
Library of Congress Cataloging-in-Publication Data
Names: Petty, Heather, author.
Title: Final fall / Heather W. Petty.
Description: First edition. | New York : Simon & Schuster Books for Young Readers, [2017]. | Series: Lock & Mori | Summary: Mori escapes captivity in the English countryside and returns to London, where she plots the downfall of her father and his cohorts but discovers that Lock may no longer be an ally.
Identifiers: LCCN 2017015758 | ISBN 9781481423090 (hardback) | ISBN 9781481423113 (eBook)
Subjects: | CYAC: Mystery and detective stories. | Characters in literature—Fiction. | Love—Fiction. | London (England)—Fiction. | England—Fiction.
Classification: LCC PZ7.1.P48 Lo 2015 | DDC [Fic]—dc23
LC record available at https://lccn.loc.gov/2017015758

To my Lumberjack—
you know why

I spent the first week of my confinement pacing my cage like a circus tiger and demanding to see my brothers at anyone who came near. I used mealtimes to gauge the passing of hours and ate as quickly as I could so I could hurl my empty plates through the bars at the heads of my captors. I thought then that I was as angry as I could get.

Then another full week went by and still I had no sign of Alice or my brothers. I knew this was my punishment for hurting Alice that first day—her face probably still showed the bruises from where I'd slammed her head against the bars of my cell. But in the darkest part of the night, I couldn't sleep for the panicked idea that maybe they'd left for America without me. That maybe, by the time I escaped, Alice would have covered their trail so well, I'd never be able to find my brothers in that giant landscape.

By week three, the two guards Alice had assigned to watch over me started playing Ro-Sham-Bo to determine who would bring me food. I'd taken to hiding in the shadows of my prison, at first with the idea that I'd lunge out and scare anyone who got too close, but they seemed more unnerved by my silence than they'd ever been by my posturing. So I slid out of sight and watched the cowards huddle close together, stare at my empty cot from over their shoulders, and play their childish games. And when the one called Lucas bent down to slide my plate under the bars, I reached through and dug my fingers into his rough, auburn curls.

I hung on with all my might and pulled his head against the bars. And when he reached his arm through them to try to stop me, I leveraged the limb back and down, twisting his shoulder unnaturally and using my weight to keep him in pain so that he was forced to press his back against the cage to get some relief. Then I slipped my free arm through the bars and around his neck.

Lucas managed to yelp out, "Help!"

The other guard ran over. "Jus' let him go. Nice and easy."

"Get me my brothers and maybe I don't snap his neck." I was pretty sure I didn't have the strength to actually hurt him all that badly, but the threat seemed to stun the nameless guard into a bit of a silent panic. Alice had apparently warned them about me. I could use that.

Lucas was doing his best to stay quiet, but when the other one took too long to decide what to do, he shouted, "Get Trent, you dullard!"

Trent was apparently their leader. That was good to know.

"Not Trent. My brothers." I put a little more weight on Lucas's oddly angled arm, until he yelped again.

"Stan! Just go!"

Stan obeyed readily enough, though I didn't expect to see my brothers come through the doors. Not really. Alice was keeping them from me on purpose. She hadn't even given me an update on Michael's condition since the night her nurse friend had tended to my wounds. All I knew was that he hadn't woken up yet, and that was supposedly normal "considering what he's gone through." That left me helpless in a cage, with Michael in a coma and my other brothers under the care of a psychopath who had killed three people and was unduly fixated on my mum. She could be doing anything to them, and there was nothing I could do to stop her.

Lucas cried out again, and I shifted my weight a bit to take some of the pressure off his arm. If I were going to break him, I'd do it in front of Alice, not before she got here.

"She's not coming," a voice said from somewhere up in the rafters of the barn.

"Who's there?" I shouted. I must have clung tighter to Lucas in my alarm, because he started to choke and his fingernails dug into the skin of my arm.

"You'll have to do better than threaten that one there to get her attention."

"Show yourself!" I held Lucas tighter still, and his breaths started to rasp in and out. He scratched and pulled at my arm some more, but he was already weakening, and something about that fascinated me.

Could I really do it? Could I hold him until he fell unconscious? Until he died?

"Now you're thinking. You've sent one guard off and

you're putting the other one out of commission. But if this was your plan all along, why'd you wait so long to do it?"

Lucas slumped unconscious in my arms and I let him drop against the bars. I immediately knelt in the dirt, feeling around his pockets for keys to my cell, while I squinted up into the shadows of the rafters looking for whoever was taunting me. It didn't really matter who he was. He was only one man, and I couldn't let him stop me. I had to get up to the farmhouse to see my brothers. I had to know they were okay.

No keys. I started to roll him over to check his other side, but then I heard a thud somewhere in the barn, and the voice came closer.

"Do you really think Miss Alice would leave the key to your freedom with a man too idiotic to use the flashlight at his belt to find you before approaching your cell?"

He was right. Alice was too smart for that. In fact, she probably wouldn't trust anyone but herself. My key was most likely hanging round her neck.

I shook away an enticing little vision of me strangling her with the chain she'd used to hold that key and then grabbed Lucas's flashlight, holding it up like a club, but turning it on to spotlight the corner of the barn from where I was sure the voice had come. He had already moved.

"Well done."

I turned to the right where a figure leaned against one of the barn's main support beams. He wore black, like the rest of the guards, but he had a short green jacket on. It was vaguely military, as was his hair, which was all buzzed around the sides and short on top. When the light hit his face, he lifted a hand to shield his eyes so that only his smile shone bright.

"You must be Trent," I said.

He didn't confirm or deny it, but I was pretty sure I was right. He had the confident swagger of a man in charge. Not at all what I expected from one of Alice's men. Younger and smarter than her usual—too smart, perhaps, to work for the likes of her.

"So, what's next in this plan of yours? You've dispatched your guards. Now what?"

"You let me out?"

He shook his head, but his smile widened. "It wouldn't matter too much if I did. I've got men posted around the perimeter. You wouldn't get far."

"I only need to get to the house."

Trent seemed to consider that. "Tell you what, I see at least four ways out of that cage of yours. If you get out on your own and can incapacitate me, I'll give you a free pass to the house."

I eyed him skeptically and then used my flashlight to take him in. He wasn't more than four or five inches taller than me, and he was mostly skinny, until I got to his shoulders, which were broad; the fabric of his jacket pulled around his arms in a few key places. He was strong. But I'd learned how to fight in a way where his strength shouldn't matter. Maybe.

"Just you? You're not going to call in more of your men?"

"Just me."

I watched him for a few seconds and then pushed my hand out between the bars. "Shake on it?"

He chuckled softly and shook his head. "You'll have to take my word for it. I'm not as easy to fool as the others."

I shrugged and turned off the flashlight, stepping back so that I could look at my cage as a whole. I'd spent three weeks in the tiny space and had been so focused on the other side of the bars, I'd done very little exploration of the cell space itself. I'd also given Alice too much credit, assumed she wouldn't put me somewhere that had a way out. I hadn't even considered until that night that I could have escaped without the key. I should've known better. Every trap has a flaw.

And mine was the toilet.

My cell was crafted from what had probably been three horse stalls at one point. The walls between them had been taken out, and the fronts of each had been replaced with a wall of bars. And then the side wall of the farthest stall had been converted into a kind of barred gate—the main way in and out. Alice had built a room to house the toilet, shower, and sink that took up most of the first stall. I thought it was odd to frame and drywall a room within a room instead of just walling off the final stall to create a separate space, but that was how it had been built. And from where I stood, it looked as though a person standing on the toilet tank could reach the top of the framed wall rather easily.

I quickly estimated the space from the toilet tank to the rafter that sliced across the open bathroom ceiling. It couldn't have been more than three or four feet. If I could somehow reach it, I thought maybe I could hoist myself up. Probably not, but it was worth a try.

My chances were better if I could get a running start, but that meant calculating which foot to start with and timing exactly when to jump from the floor onto the toilet seat and then up onto the tank, so I'd have enough momentum to climb up the sparse drywall behind it. It was an impossible trick, the kind that only worked in action films after careful choreography and several scene takes. But something about Trent's challenge had lit a spark in me. He was most likely messing with me—playing another of Alice's mind games, perhaps. But if there was even a sliver of a chance, I had to try. I had to know that my brothers were okay.

"Easiest way out first," I said, then shook the bars of the gate. I grabbed at the padlock on the other side and pulled down, but it just clicked uselessly. I turned to lean my back against the gate and sighed, then pretended to look around. If I could get up into the rafters quickly enough, I thought maybe I could let myself down again on the other side and run out the front barn door before Trent could catch on.

I was pretty sure that was a pipe dream, but still I waited, staring at the ground until I had completely mapped out the run in my head. And then I ran, left foot first so that my step up onto the toilet lid with my right launched me up. I barely tapped the tank with my left foot for added momentum, but only managed to hook my fingers over the top of the wall for all my running start. I scrambled up the wall, and by the time I managed to pull myself up enough to plant a knee on the top edge, I saw Trent's head pop up into the rafters just a few feet away from me.

"Not the easiest way, but effective."

He disappeared and I scowled, hopping up onto the nearest beam. I'd made it into the rafters, and now I was stuck there, with no way to get down or past him. And the rafters wobbled a bit when I stepped from one to the other. They seemed sturdy enough to hold me, but moved just enough to make me feel like I could fall at any second. Still, I walked across them until I found hay bales stacked high enough to act like a ladder for when I was ready to climb down. But first I needed to find a way out of the barn.

I looked around as best I could but didn't see Trent anywhere. A bad sign, I was sure, but sitting in the rafters wasn't going to make him appear or make my escape any cleaner. So I started to climb down. At the last minute, before my toes could brush the dirt floor, I saw a flash of movement in my periphery, and then the lights went out. I climbed up and over another nearby bale of hay, setting myself down on the far side. The tantalizing glow of the moon shone in through the doors from the outside, which left me two options: run for it and hope that Trent didn't expect me to be that bold, or play hide-and-seek for a while until I could find an opening to escape past him.

I ran for the barn doors. I could hear Trent's footsteps not far behind me, but luck was on my side. A trunk of riding equipment almost sent me sprawling, and when I caught myself, my hand brushed against a riding crop sticking out by the back hinge. It wasn't much of a weapon, but it was something. Maybe Lock's Bartitsu lessons wouldn't turn out to be completely useless.

With Trent close enough that I could hear his breathing, I spun to face him, holding the crop in both hands in front of me. He didn't even pause. Before I could use my weapon to stop him, his hand was on my arm. In the next second I was completely in his control, both of my arms held behind my back by just one of his. I spent a few hopeful moments struggling against his grip, but then stopped. It was useless. He had me.

He pushed my hand up my back, pressing at my elbow until my shoulder ached. It was an unnecessary precaution. Probably more of a message than an attempt to injure. But it freed up his other hand to pull something from around his neck as he walked me back to my cell. He had a key too, which was good to know, and he didn't seem overly concerned about his men. Or maybe he was truly cross with Lucas, because he nudged his unconscious body aside as if he were an errant bale of hay.

After he'd unlocked the padlock, he shoved me up against the bars like he needed to get a better hold on me. "The middle child is awake," he said quietly. "And the oldest sneaks out at night."

"She giving you trouble there, Trent?" Stan had apparently returned.

"This little thing?" Trent mocked, loudly. "Trouble to me?" And then in a whisper he said, "Two a.m. North corner," and pushed me inside my cell so that I stumbled and fell to my knees. "She was apparently too much for Lucas, though. Come make sure he isn't dead?"

Stan laughed, and I hid my face like I was ashamed, to keep them from seeing my satisfaction. I'd managed to find an informant at least. And our deal was still on as far as I could tell. If I could beat Trent somehow, I'd get a free pass to the house. To Michael. All I needed was a plan.

Two plans. One to escape and another to neutralize Alice once and for all. I'd only get one shot at her, I was sure about that.

Chapter 2

According to Trent, there were three more ways out of my cell, and I was determined to find them all before my next tussle with the man. That meant it was time to explore.

I went to the north corner of the cell first. An odd little cove had been created between the bathroom structure and the north-facing barn wall. There was nothing remarkable about the space, however, other than how hidden it was from the main barn area. When I inched my way to the back corner, none of the men in the barn could see me. None of the light from the overhead lamps seemed to penetrate the space either. That could prove useful.

And it was possibly one of my other ways up into the rafters. The back wall of the bathroom was smooth enough that with my back pressed up against it and my feet pushing against the rough barn siding, I could walk my way up the side pretty readily. I tried it, still hidden from the guards, and about halfway up found a crossbeam of the bathroom framing that was just wide enough for me to sit on. As carefully as I could, I twisted my body to bring my feet up, then slowly stood on the beam. At that height, I could see a rafter just inches above the bathroom wall. It was a perfect escape, really, which meant no one could ever find out about it, or they'd find a way to block it off for sure.

Satisfied, I hopped back down, then wandered out toward my cot just as Stan brought his and Lucas's dinner trays. "No luck on the hazard pay," Stan said. His expression was practically bursting with amusement. "Trent said he should dock your pay for sleepin' on the job!"

Stan laughed and Lucas glared over at the corner where I'd been hiding before. Which was when I saw that I'd dropped his flashlight there by the door, and no one had noticed.

I coughed to distract him, and waved my fingers a little when he turned toward the noise. He subconsciously ran a hand over his hair, and then scowled and tucked into his meal. I took advantage of their distraction to fetch the flashlight and hide it back in the little alcove I'd found in the north corner of my cell. And then I sat there for a while and listened to my guards eat like hogs at a trough, while gazing around my hiding place, positioning myself to spy on what bits of my cell I could see from there.

Unfortunately, the space wasn't designed for reconnaissance. I could only see a few bars and a bit of the swung-open bathroom door. Which was when I realized that the door was oddly shaped. It was ancient looking, with worn wood and peeling red paint that looked to have once been the color of the painted brick by the barn entrance. Like maybe it had been a main barn door. It had to be at least seven feet tall, so if I could just get it off the hinges, it could easily become a ramp to take me up and over the top of the stall walls, where the top framing of the bars gave way to open rafters.

When my guards finally turned down the lamps for the night and things got quiet, I peeked around the edge of the door. Lucas was standing at the gate with his back to the cell, and Stan was nowhere to be seen, though I could hear him chatting with someone near the entrance to the barn itself. I clicked on the flashlight and peered around the corner again. No one seemed to notice the light. I slid the light beam along the hinged seam of the door.

The top two hinges seemed painted shut and would take some work to unstick, but the bottom one looked new. Before I could look at it too closely, I was distracted by something carved along the edge of the door. I had to practically lie down on the straw-covered floor to see it properly, but there, along the bottom, near the corner, was a tiny carved message:

IF ANYONE SEES THIS, MY NAME IS
ALICE STOKES
HELD CAPTIVE 223 DAYS
2 NOV 90

So Alice hadn't built this prison, she'd been victim to it, and for much longer than I had. I might have laughed, but the flashlight shifted as I pushed myself back up onto my knees, displaying rather plainly Alice's little calendar of sorts. She'd etched marks into the wood, and there were many, many more than 223. If each of the marks truly represented a day of Alice's imprisoned teen years, it was a miracle she could function at all. That door represented well over eighteen months of confinement.

I might have felt pity for her if she hadn't turned around and done the same to me. But that begged the question, why had she been confined? And, more importantly, what did she expect this captivity would do to me?

With those questions and several more swirling through my thoughts, I expected I'd never be able to sleep that night. But just in case, I crawled back into the alcove and waited for two a.m.

It took about thirty seconds too long for my sleep-addled brain to figure out why it was so cramped and dark and what was making that irritating thunking noise right by my head.

"What is it?" I groaned, perhaps more loudly than I should have.

Everything got quiet for a few heartbeats, and then I heard the growling breaths and outright snores of my night watch. Moments later, two of the boards in the wall were dragged aside, leaving a small, screened opening right at the north corner. I switched on the flashlight and gasped.

"Freddie!" I managed to keep my voice low, but I couldn't help the tears that formed in my eyes. It hadn't been a month without him, and still I felt a rush of relief on seeing him.

"It's you," he said, pushing his fingers up against the screen.

I pressed my fingers against his and felt a tear trace down

my cheek, which I quickly wiped away. It wasn't the same as having him with me in my cell, but I could feel the warmth of his skin.

"Trent said I should throw rocks against this panel and then slide it over. I didn't think . . ."

"That I'd be on the other side? I had no idea why he told me to be here either. But I needed to see you. I've been throwing a fit about it."

"I've been going out at night to look for you, but I couldn't get into the barn because of all the men around it. Should've known that's where you'd be. Are you locked in there?"

"Never mind about me. How are you three? Tell me everything."

"Sean's fine. He's Alice's favorite, so he gets to do anything he wants. He even gets to learn fighting from Trent."

"But not you?"

Freddie made a face. "Too busy."

I was pretty sure there was more to that story, but I let it go. "And Michael?"

Fred stared at the ground and wouldn't look up.

"What is it? You have to tell me."

"Alice says we aren't to tell you that."

"Since when do you listen to Alice over me?"

"She says it's for your own good. To keep you from becoming like Dad."

I felt my lip curl at the mention of our father, at Alice's comparison of me to him. "She knows nothing."

"She says—"

"Alice doesn't get a say. She isn't our family."

I watched his little face cloud over in thought, then clear again. He leaned in close to the screen, practically brushing the metal with his lips. He wasn't smiling.

"He's different, Mori. Like a different person. And he doesn't remember things."

My heart sped up, fueled by some overdosing combination of terror and rage. "But he's still recovering, right? He'll get better once he heals."

Freddie winced away from what he was about to tell me. "That's what the nurse says to us, but not what she says to Alice."

"In private?" I asked, though I knew the answer.

"When she thinks we aren't around."

Suddenly nothing else seemed to matter. I needed to see Michael. I needed to see for myself.

"Go back to the house."

"I've got a little time to talk still."

"Go back. I'll meet you there."

Fred stared at me a moment, and then I heard the soft scraping sound of the boards moving back into place, but I was up and moving before they closed.

Pushing my back against the outer bathroom wall, I kicked my feet up against the barn siding and leveraged myself to walk up. It felt like a much longer journey this time, maybe because I was trying to keep a flashlight balanced on my lap while I moved. Maybe because I was pausing more to make sure all my little scraping and stepping sounds hadn't woken up someone who'd be ready to catch me on the other side of the bars. I couldn't have that. Not tonight.

When I was standing on the framing beam, I set the flashlight up on a rafter, then pulled myself up next to it. I'd done it. All was quiet and sleeping sounds on the ground floor, so I let myself flash the light on twice. Once to make sure of my path across the ceiling rafters and another to find footholds and handles that let me climb down a support column right by the front barn doors.

I briefly wondered what Trent would have thought of this little performance, but then turned my focus to my next obstacle: how to get from the barn to the house without being seen. Through the open door, I could see a few soft lights in the main house, but there was no movement between the barn and those lights. I thought I could make out a few figures down the drive toward the front gate, but none near me—at least, none of the ones surrounding the barn that Freddie had warned me about.

It was a risk, but I knew I didn't have much time. I'd have to run for it and hope Trent's perimeter men weren't looking for me between the barn and the house. If I could run in bursts and keep out of the moonlight, I'd be okay.

I made it all the way to the lush garden before I saw another guard. I wasn't sure of his name, though I thought I'd heard Stan say it once. Grady, was it? Grady the guard? He was a big one, but somehow less imposing than the others. Maybe it was that he was only an inch or two taller than me. I hunkered down by a great tower of snap peas and waited for him to pass. He seemed to stare up at the barn for a little too long, then started to jog toward it.

I didn't have time to care about what he had seen. I had to get to Michael. So the minute he was gone, I made sure there wasn't another pair of eyes staring me down from the darkness, and then I ran as fast as I could for the side kitchen door that Alice had taken me through just a few months ago. Back when she was just the blue-haired lady from my mum's picture. Back when she was my mum's friend and our care-taker. Before I knew what she'd really become.

I was at once surprised and not surprised to find the door unlocked. We were in the very definition of countryside, where people rarely locked their houses, or so I'd been told. Still, Alice's paranoia made me suspicious of how easy she'd made it for anyone to enter the place where she slept. But when an eager white face popped up to fill one of the glass panes of the kitchen door, I knew not to worry.

Freddie had unlocked it. He smiled, then pulled the door open and jumped into my arms. It was an odd gesture from my oldest brother. He wasn't overly stoic, but he wasn't one for sentimentality either. I couldn't think of a time in our lives when he'd hugged me that way. But knowing he was okay and knowing he'd been worried for me too made me wish he'd never let go.

I held him as tight as I could for a few seconds, then gently pushed him away. I whispered, "Don't want to get caught out here." I looked around just to make my point, which was when I saw lights up at the barn. "We don't have too much time now."

Freddie straightened up and nodded, then grabbed my hand and pulled me deeper into the house. It wasn't a palatial estate, just a long ranch house, with a string of rooms leading to a long hall with more rooms. And Michael's room was of course at the farthest end. But we reached it too soon, or at least that was how it felt. With my hand on the doorknob, I felt suddenly numb, like I wasn't ready to see what was on the other side. Still, I opened the door.

Chapter 3

What I saw was anticlimactic. Michael slept alone in his bed, and all the medical equipment that had apparently traveled with him to this place was pushed off into a corner. The only clues to his affliction were his fluffy curls shaved down to almost nothing and the stark white headband that held some gauze to the side of his head.

I sat next to him and gave myself a moment to take him in, to listen to his breathing, to see that he wasn't all that different from before. But then he opened his eyes.

"MORI!"

Fred and I shushed him at the same time, which only served to make him laugh.

"Mori," he whispered playfully as he clambered out of bed. He turned to Fred. "She's my sister. I told you I remember the important things."

I saw a joyous light shining in his eyes, one that I'd never seen in him before. He'd always been so alert, watching for danger and ready to cower from it. But his vigilance also made him anxious for the ones he loved, concerned and ready to stand by them. Now he seemed free of all of that. Carefree. And even though I should have been happy to see him so relaxed, I couldn't help but yearn for the frightened little boy who still needed to climb up into my lap when he was scared. Maybe he'd never be frightened again, but did that also mean he'd lost his ability to assess his surroundings properly? Would he never again be the clever, most observant boy in our family? Had we really lost him for good?

I noticed I had tears in my eyes when Michael looked at the night-light by the door and tilted his head. "It's got a halo," he said. "Like an angel."

And in the next second, he went stiff as a board and started to deadfall back to the floor. I caught him and managed to help him down so that he didn't injure himself further. But he wouldn't respond to his name, and his whole body started to convulse.

"Get the nurse!" I cried.

But Freddie hesitated. "They'll find you and take you away again."

"It doesn't matter," I said. "I'll find another way out. Now go!"

He ran off and I was left with my helplessness and ignorance. I had no idea what Michael needed. All I could do was keep watch over his head and hope this wasn't the end of his life. That I hadn't somehow caused this.

But I knew better than that. I knew exactly who had caused this.

I made a list as I knelt by my brother's body, his limbs tensing and flailing in equal measure. The names filtered through my grief to etch into my mind forever—all the people who had contributed to that moment, whether through negligence, ignorance, or loyalty. The list was my crusade, but it all centered around one name. And I realized rather quickly that my true revenge couldn't start until that name was erased from my list, from my thoughts, from the planet.

James Moriarty.

My name. His name. And before I was done, there would be only one of us left breathing.

I was so entrenched in my rage that when the tiny doll of a thing that was Alice's nurse friend appeared at the door, I could only growl, "Fix him!"

Whether she was surprised to see me there or angry to be ordered about by a teenager didn't filter into her expression. She was entirely focused on Michael from the moment she stepped in the room, and of the four of us, she was definitely the one in charge.

"On his side," she said, spurring me to action.

She dragged a metal cart from the corner to the bed and had a syringe in her hand before I could turn a still-flailing Michael onto his side. She pushed the drug into his hip and then helped me hold him there until his seizing subsided. Only then did our eyes meet. "If you have questions, ask now before Alice finds you," she said.

"Did I cause this?"

She shook her head. "Probably not. There are lots of triggers. Common enough for him to have a few seizures during his recovery."

"Will he always have them?"

"Maybe. Maybe not. It's impossible to tell right now."

"But he's still healing? He could get better?"

The nurse met my eyes and laid a hand on my shoulder. "There was brain damage, but we can't know how much will heal and how much won't. He might not ever go back to how he was. Not completely."

I ran my fingers through the sweaty hairs at his temple, then found the nurse's gaze again. "If I find a way out, if I can pay you, will you come with us?"

"He shouldn't travel now. He needs time to heal."

"But when he's ready? Will you help us?"

She sighed, clearly conflicted. "I'll work on that from my end. If I can't go, I'll find someone who can. Now you'd better get back before—"

"Where is she? And why is Michael's light on?!"

We were too late. It was all I could do to lift Michael's still-unconscious body back up onto his bed before Alice, Stan, and Trent were rushing through the doorway. I had started to straighten Michael's bedclothes over him, when Alice tried to push between me and the bed to get to him.

"What have you done to my—?"

I slammed her up against the wall, my arm across her neck and an open sneer tightening my lips across bared teeth. "He's not *your* anything," I ground out.

Alice tried to respond, but she just gasped and gaped at me instead. My arm was pressing on her throat too hard, and I knew it, but I couldn't seem to make myself stop. I didn't want to. Just then, I wanted to keep watching her eyes grow wider with terror. I wanted her to fear me more than anything in her life.

Stan came at me, and when he got close enough, I punched out as hard as I could at his sternum. It was a lucky shot, but it sent him back a few steps, enough to collide with Trent and give me a couple of more seconds with Alice. I stared into her eyes.

"Next time I get out, I'm coming straight for your worthless life." I leaned in close enough to smell the sweat on her. "So be good, Aunt Alice. Let us go now and I'll spare you."

I was yanked off her by two giant hands that pulled my arms behind my back. I kicked out, but only managed to tag poor Stan in the shoulder again.

"You can't keep me locked up forever!" I screamed as Trent dragged me from the room and down the hall. Seanie came out of his room just as I was pulled around the corner, and I heard him yell my name, heard his running steps chase after me. But I only got one more glimpse of him being held back by Freddie as I was torn from the house and tossed out onto the dewy front lawn. I jumped up and ran back toward the house, but Trent pushed me back again, harder this time so that I lost my balance and fell onto the grass. I started to get up, but I was surrounded by a forest of legs, all attached to Trent's guards, with no path through.

"Are you done with your tantrum now?" Trent barked at me. He leaned over, bracing his hands on his knees while trying to catch his breath.

I lay on my back and stared up at the sky, my own breaths

coming in stuttered hiccups. Giant hot tears fell down my temples and into my hair, and I didn't even try to stop them. I felt so heavy, like I could feel the gravity pulling me into the earth. My heart was heavy too, because Alice had beaten me yet again. No matter how many times I lashed out or screamed, no matter how many of her guards I incapacitated, I was stuck there until Michael was healthy enough to travel. We were all stuck there, and I couldn't protect my brothers from inside a cage.

When Trent finally lumbered back over to where I was, there was pity in his eyes, though not enough, it seemed, to leave me to my moment on the lawn. Or maybe he thought it more merciful to take me away from all the men who still stood in a circle around me, gaping at the spectacle. He hauled me up to my feet and used both of his hands on my shoulders to walk me back toward the barn.

We'd almost reached the garden when I composed myself enough to whisper, "Help us."

"I can't, so don't ask again."

"I just want to take them and go. I'll leave Alice alone if you let us leave."

Trent cursed under his breath and then shouted, "Stop fighting me!" He pinned my arms behind me again, then spoke quietly at the back of my head. "These men here are all for the money. And she's promised them double once she escapes to America with you and those boys in tow."

"And you? Do you get triple?"

Trent redirected me into the garden area, then released me

so that I stumbled forward two steps. I turned on him, putting my hands up to fight, but thought better of it the minute I saw his stormy expression. "I get my freedom," he said.

My hopes fell to dust. She had something on him. Something big. "What did you do?"

Trent dusted off his hands and stared up at the barn. "Doesn't matter. All you need to know is that I can't help you leave."

"Then why did you help me earlier? With Fred?"

Trent tried to ignore me. He put his hands back on my shoulders and turned me toward the barn. "Let's go."

I thought I'd been so clever escaping out of the cage, finding such a large gap in the guards who usually surrounded the barn. Only it hadn't been me at all. Trent had let me go to the house, let me see my brothers, but that was as far as his help would go. "Do you want to help us leave?"

"Doesn't matter what I want, so let's go."

I turned to face him. "I'll find a way."

Trent tried to turn me around again, but I wouldn't budge.

"Listen. I won't ask you to help us escape. But if I can find a way to get us out without implicating you, would you look the other way at least?"

He raised a brow and crossed his arms, but he wasn't pushing us to move, so that was something.

"Or you could let me kill her and you'd be free just the same."

Trent shook his head. "Can't let you kill her."

He should've wanted her dead. Should have and could

have killed her himself, and whatever she had on him would die with her. There was only one reason why he'd want to keep her alive. "If she dies, your secret is revealed?"

He stared at me in a different way then, like he wasn't sure I couldn't read his mind or something. But he didn't know that was my mum's old trick. My mum's crew had set up a system of sending letters out to one another when they died so that the money they'd earned together would never be lost should anything happen to one of them. No doubt Alice had taken out a similar insurance policy to keep herself breathing.

Trent never affirmed nor denied whether my guess was true, but I knew I was right when an expression of disgust filtered over his features as he turned me around and marched me back toward the barn. He didn't say another word until I was in my cage, and even then it was only to tell me to step away from the gate. But I didn't do as he said. I stayed right next to the bars, staring at him while he secured the lock. And I reached out to grab his hand before he could pull away.

When he looked up at me, I said, "I'll find a way."

"Find a way to what?" Alice asked, and the very sound of her voice made my whole body tense.

I hadn't heard her come into the barn, but I should have known she'd be out to gloat eventually. It was all I could do not to lunge through the bars for her again, but I managed to restrain myself. I withdrew my hand from Trent's and turned to face her.

"To escape? Not if you want to see your brothers again."

I clenched my jaw to keep from speaking and drew my

hands into fists to keep still. I wasn't going to give her the satisfaction of seeing my true turmoil. Trent started to leave, but Alice held up a hand to make him stay.

"Do you remember when I taught you about priming a mark, Mori? That you give them what they want and then they give you a favor in return?" Alice's smile was almost predatory. "You just became my mark."

I kept myself steady only because I knew she was wrong. What was that she'd said all those weeks ago? When you do it right, the mark never knows he was conned? Well, I knew. And I wasn't so easily cowed by her.

"What do you want?"

"It's not about what I want. It's what you want that matters here." Alice let her fingers trail across the bars as she walked toward us, but I noticed that the nearer she got to me, the farther she retreated from the bars. When she finally faced me, she grinned. "You shouldn't have come to the house, sweetie. You gave away what you want."

My brothers. It wasn't some great reveal, but she was right. I had shown how much those boys were my weakness. What she obviously didn't know was that they were also my strength. For them, I could burn this whole place down with her screaming inside and never look back. Just the thought of it brought a smile to my lips.

"You let me see my brothers and then I do you a favor in return?"

Alice nodded. "So smart, our Mori."

"What's your favor?"

"I need a soldier," she said. "I need someone I can trust to play warrior by my side—to be my sword. Trent here is going to train you to do that."

"You think you can trust me?"

"Of course I can, Mori. Because I have what you want. And if you want to see your brothers, you'll train to fight for me."

"And if I don't?"

Alice paused for effect, and I tried very hard not to roll my eyes at her dramatics. "America is a very big place. If we go there without you . . ."

She'd done it. Somehow Alice had discovered my greatest fear, the one thing that made these bars feel like they were closing in on me. I couldn't lose my brothers. Not like that. Not to her.

And I wouldn't. She wanted to train me to be a soldier? Fine, but she was only crafting the weapon that would destroy her. I'd play along, but I'd be no one's mark. Not for long, anyway. Let her think she'd won just up until the moment I was strong enough to beat her game. Then we'd walk free from that place, my brothers and me, hopefully while she watched, helpless to stop us.

My expression must have given away something Alice had wanted to see just then, because she gave me a satisfied smile and turned to leave. "Your training starts tomorrow."

Yes, it does, I thought in return.

Chapter 4

Four months later . . .

Margaret Atwood once wrote, "Oh, if revenge did move the stars instead of love, they would not shine."

She was wrong about that.

Then why did you pick that quote for tonight? That's what Lock would've asked, were he in Piddinghoe.

Because I can see the stars, would be my reply. *The stars made me think of the quote. But she's wrong.*

Is she?

For months my every thought has been about revenge, and still the stars shine. At least, what I could see of them through the small open hatch in the roof of my horse-stall prison. Not even the pulsing dark images of my father lying dead in a pool of his own blood and Alice kneeling and weeping over her unending ruin could mute their twinkling light.

And if Lock were in the barn with me, by now he'd be fully entranced in one of his ridiculous experiments, ignoring me completely. Or perhaps lost in a book? His fingers forming the chords of a song on his violin so that the melody played in his mind, even when he never lifted his bow? And if he spoke, if he made any noise at all, it would be some mono-syllabic sound meant to make me believe he was listening when it was clear he was not.

Hmh.

Even my pretend version of Lock was annoyingly noncommittal.

You agree that she's wrong.

Obviously, though not for the reasons you give.

Do enlighten.

My pretend Lock looked at me with a raised brow. *Stars move because of gravity. It has nothing at all to do with human emotion.*

Atwood's was another failed quote, then. I was losing the game.

"And losing my mind," I whispered into the darkness, turning my head so that my imaginary Lock would fade away.

I'd thought the physical constraints of Alice's prison would be the hardest to survive over the months she'd held me captive in the countryside, but that wasn't true. The sameness of every day was what clawed at my sanity. The schedule of it. The mind-numbing doldrums of set feedings, visitations, and training sessions, and the endless spaces between those events where I had nothing but my own mind to entertain me—that was what I could barely survive.

So I'd created all these little games to fill the gaps. And a version of Sherlock Holmes to play them with me. The quote game I mostly played at night. I would rest a hand against the wall so that my thumb could trace the gouges I'd made on my first day there. Perfect little divots that represented all the promises I'd made to myself—one, to escape this cell; two, to make my brothers safe; three, to remove the threat of Alice and my father, and four . . .

Four didn't matter.

But with those marks and my revenge at the forefront of my daily thoughts, I'd stare up at the rough square of sky I could see and let my mind float through all the words I'd read and heard in my schooling, trying to find a quote to fit my day and circumstances. Imaginary Lock always seemed to have something to say about whichever quote I chose. Never anything helpful, though.

"Gravity," I said bitterly.

Recently we'd had three days in a row without rain, which was probably why my mind had settled around quotes about stars that night. Stars that I could barely see—and still I could see more of them than I'd ever seen in London. Not that the night sky would ever be enough to keep me from yearning for home.

I could envision myself there, walking the streets of my city, surrounded by hundreds of pedestrians, the slow-moving traffic ebbing by. Nighttime in Regent's Park and the luring scent of cloves emanating from the soft orange glow of Lock sneaking a drag in the shadows of my bandstand. Not a star in the sky. Just the radiant city lights.

"If revenge did move the stars instead of love," I said. And then I smiled. Maybe Ms. Atwood was right. London would be the place of my revenge, after all.

I'd scarcely let visions of me stalking my father through the streets of London settle into my mind when I heard the soft squeak of a board shifting against its nails. And then I couldn't see any stars at all, which meant it had begun—the test.

I rolled off my cot just as a giant ball of netting fell down from the crossbeams above, unfurling to capture the now-empty space where I'd just been. I took advantage of the *thwump* of its fall to take cover in the corner by the bathroom that faced the barred gate. The bathroom had a roof now, and a canvas flap instead of a door—both part of Alice's response to the various escape attempts I'd made whenever she'd kept me from my brothers for longer than I deemed acceptable. But they still hadn't found my escape route through the alcove, and I wasn't about to show them during a skills test.

That left only one way out—through the gate.

I started running the second I heard the click of the padlock so that by the time the gate slammed open I was crouched down beside it. Tonight's sparring partner sprang into my cell and stood there like an idiot, legs parted in the stance Lucas always took when he thought he got the jump on me. Ridiculous man. I slid through the opening behind him, pulled the gate closed, and clicked shut the padlock, trapping him inside. Then I turned to glance around for my actual foe. I saw two figures by the door, but neither were Trent. He'd doubled the guard that night, though, which had to mean he knew I had a chance to beat him. That was all I needed, a chance.

I rolled into the shadows, then used an upright bale of hay and a cast-iron lamp hanger to scurry up one of the barn's support columns and into the rafters above. From there I could see them all—two of Alice's men guarding the exit, and Lucas scouring every inch of the cell for me. He hadn't even noticed he was locked in yet.

I crawled slowly back into the slant of the roof and waited to find my opening. The wait was the hardest part of this little drill. My muscles were tense, heated from the paces I'd already put them through in my before-bed exercise routine. Adrenaline pumped through me, begging me to do something—anything. And somehow I had to stay still and silent, balanced precariously in the dusty space between the roof and my beam. All I could do was watch.

I found Trent squeezed between a supply cabinet and wall stud near the main barn door, like he'd expected me to make a blatant run for it, like I hadn't learned that lesson weeks ago. I was mostly sure I'd only seen him because he'd allowed it. The hideout was so well crafted, I briefly wondered how many times I'd run past it looking for my own place to hide.

Even though he could have spied me from where he was, he took two steps forward, peering into every space large enough to house my form. His gaze turned upward then, landing first on the rafter where he'd found me the night before. He took a step back to look at the beams where he'd given himself away by hiding my stars. And though I knew his next step would give him a perfect view of me, I shifted my gaze away from him for a second or two, sure that something had moved near his original hideout. But no matter how I willed my vision to pierce the dim, there was nothing. No more movement. Not even the shine of eyes.

"Well done, lass," Trent said from almost directly below me. I'd been so focused on chasing ghosts while straining to hear the whispering sounds of his steps on the hay-covered floorboards, his voice sounded like shouting in my ears. I jerked my head toward the sound, and found him staring up at me. He lifted his arm to check his watch while keeping me in his sights. "No record tonight, though. Three minutes? You haven't given yourself away this quickly in a month."

"Seeing me isn't catching me, old man."

And then the chase was on. The bastard was up in the rafters before I could cross halfway to the other side, but I was faster jumping the beams. I lowered myself between two near the corner and landed on a soft pile of hay that had come loose from a bale. But I didn't have time to rest. I slithered through the shadowed maze of stacked bales, saddle stands, and workbenches until an opening and a stall wall forced me out into the center of the main barn. I backed into a corner, but Trent's thudding steps in my direction told me all my attempts at stealth had been for naught.

Weapons. I'd run past tables full of them like an idiot, and the only thing I had in reach now was an old shop broom. Keeping as still as I could, I turned the handle to loosen it from the bristle base. The squeak of the wood as it turned sounded like a scream, alerting everyone of my location, but it didn't matter. He knew exactly where I was.

Thankfully, I knew where he was as well and ducked down

to yank the handle free just as he threw his first punch. I felt his fist swish by my face and dropped lower to keep his elbow from connecting. I heard Lucas rattle the bars of my cage as I slammed the broom handle into the back of Trent's left knee, dropping him down to where I was kneeling. Then I jabbed one end toward his face, but I misjudged my space, and the back of the handle slapped against a support column, sending the shock of the impact through my body.

Trent paused just long enough to make me sure he was indulging in some kind of gloating smile, which was the only reason he didn't capture me right then and there. I didn't have another head shot, but I managed to knock his arm away and found my footing again. I hopped up on a workbench and used a loose piece of siding to hoist myself up in the rafters once more before he could recover.

Lucas had found a way out of my cell by then and stomped around the barn, pushing aside bales of hay and boxes and anything else I might've hid behind. His search was crude and ridiculous, but not quite useless. It did well enough to distract me. I lost precious seconds watching him when I should have kept moving, and by the time I caught myself, Trent was only two rafters from where I was balanced.

Still, if Trent could use Lucas, so could I.

I held on to the rafter and lowered myself down just enough to hang there. "Lucas! She's over here!" I whisper-shouted.

As expected, he ran toward the sound of my voice. I pulled my feet up until he was right under me, then let go so that I landed on his back. I immediately pushed off, ready to use

Lucas as a shield for when Trent inevitably dropped from the rafters somewhere near us, but Trent never showed. Which meant he was definitely up to something.

Still, that left me Lucas to deal with, and either he was quicker on his game that night or he clobbered me by mistake. But somehow his fist connected with my jaw as he turned, which made me stumble into a stack of hay. My ear started to ring and my jaw ached, but I smiled through the pain, just like Trent had taught me.

In one of our first lessons, he'd said, "Two keys to winning a fight: stamina and learning to take a hit. If you can smile through the pain and keep standing up, you've a better chance to win, even if the other guy's bigger than you."

I'd taken seven punches that day, surprising my new teacher and myself, which made Lucas's half-assed hit feel almost playful. But his second hit wouldn't be, so I shook the ringing from my head and licked the blood from my split lip. When Lucas rushed me, I used the bindings on the hay to brace myself, lifted both legs, and kicked him as hard as I could in the chest. He stumbled back a few steps and I ran forward, following up with another kick to the sternum, so that he went down hard, breaking through an old, broken saddle stand in the process.

I knew he wouldn't stay down for long, and I was preparing to face him again, when I heard a soft groan over by the main doors. I started to run for a workbench, planning to duck behind it to get my bearings, but Trent appeared on the other side before I reached it. Thankfully, I was right. Lucas didn't stay down long. Before either of us could make a move, Lucas stumbled between us, his back to me.

"Where'd she go?" he asked Trent.

"Thanks, Luc," I said into the back of the poor man's head. "I owe you." And then I swept Lucas's legs, destroying his already precarious balance, and pushed him into Trent. The two fell in a painful heap on the floor, with Lucas taking the worst of it, but I didn't stick around to see how he fared. With a soundtrack of growling and grunting as the men disentangled themselves, I ran for where I'd left my broomstick. Which meant I was ready when Trent staggered toward me.

I could've cracked his skull with my stick had I wanted to. But I still needed Trent alive, and besides, I'd come to like the man. So instead of using my weapon to strike him, I jumped aside at the last minute and used it to guide him right into one of the rusted-out toolboxes under the workbench. He still might have cracked his skull, I supposed. But I couldn't worry about that. The important part was that he didn't move.

I'd finally won!

"'These violent delights have violent ends,'" I said, smiling down at his crumpled body. I wiped a drop of blood from the corner of my mouth with my thumb. "Shakespeare. His worst play and it's still a better fit than the Atwood."

My satisfied sigh was lost in the sound of a loud conversation outside.

"What? And you're only telling me now?!"

Alice's shout sent the other guards in the barn into a frenzy, but when the lights came on, everyone froze in place. Trent wasn't the only prone figure on the dirt floor of the barn. His arm had flopped out in such a way that it appeared to be pointing at another figure, clothed in black like the rest of the guards and lying completely still in the dust.

No one else moved, so I crept closer, still cognizant of Alice's shouts just on the other side of the barn door. I rolled the man onto his back, only to find that the whole front of his jacket was wet. When I lifted my hand, I saw blood. When I lifted my gaze, I saw the deep cut along his neck.

"Grady," I whispered.

I didn't suppose anyone heard me say the name of the dead man over the scolding entrance of Alice Stokes. "Where is Trent? And what the hell is she doing out of her cell?"

Exactly two seconds later, Alice screamed.

Chapter 5

By the time Trent woke up and figured out what had happened, I was in my cell drying my newly washed hands with a towel. Trent crawled over to lean against my bars, though he still held his head, clearly in pain. Everyone else stood around Grady's body, like they thought that staring at it long enough would somehow help them figure out how the hell it got there. Alice, of course, jumped immediately to the most unreasonable conclusion.

"You did this!" She pointed an accusatory digit at me, and I offered two by way of reply, then shoved the netting aside and plopped down on my cot. "Another one of your escape attempts? Only this time you went too far?"

"It's not the girl," Trent growled. "There wasn't time for her to kill a man while she was running from me."

"Running *at* you, you mean." I shouldn't have opened my mouth.

"You had blood on your hands!" Alice accused, though her heart wasn't in it.

I blew my hair out of my eyes and gazed longingly at the

divots I'd scratched into my wall. I hadn't even fulfilled one of my promises yet. Not one. And tonight felt like a very good night to escape this place forever.

"Why was she running from you?" Alice shouted next.

Trent brought his hands up to his head. "It was just sparring."

"Which I won."

"In the dark? I told you to train her, not let her out of her cage in the pitch black so you can lose track of her." Alice took a side step away from my bars, which I was pretty sure was subconscious.

Trent shrugged. "What kind of soldier only gets his training in the light of day?"

"The kind that has threatened to kill me more than once."

Trent glanced at me and I grinned as widely as I could manage with a split lip. He shook his head and shifted so his back was to me again.

"I have the barn surrounded when we spar. She can't escape."

"She beat you. How long until she breaks through your guards?"

Trent stood and brushed dust off his jeans. "You said you wanted a sword." He gestured toward me. "You're welcome."

I heard running steps and sat up just as Stan reached Alice. He whispered something that made her go pale, and she grabbed the bars and stared at me. "Tell me it was you." When I didn't answer, she let her hands drop back to her side. "It has to be you."

She was terrified, which felt like an overreaction to one dead guard. Something else was wrong.

"Why?" I asked. I glanced over and saw the guards covering Grady's body with a tarp.

"If it's not you, then the rumors are true, and—"

The sound of my name cut off the rest of her words, and soon I was surrounded by all three of my brothers and their endless questions.

"Why is there a net on the floor?"

"What's under that tarp over there?"

"Can't everyone hear you peeing in here?"

"When are you going to come live with us at the house?"

I wanted to answer everything and revel in their visit, but Alice had dragged Trent away from my prison and I needed to hear what she would say to him.

"You three go hide in the spot I showed you last time. I'll be there in a minute."

"I call the flashlight," Seanie said, running off first. The others followed, jockeying for position, with Michael in the rear, laughing in that new, unfamiliar way he had that tore at my restraint.

"Stop pretending like I'm the one who needs to calm down!" Alice seemed to have a better handle on herself, despite the yelling. "Do you think this is a coincidence? And now, of all times!"

I inched forward enough to be able to hear and see both of them. Trent seemed calm, despite the pacing and ranting of his boss.

"Someone in the village saw him. And if what you say is true, that she couldn't have done this, then someone from the outside came in and killed one of my men! It has to be him."

"One of *my* men," Trent countered. "And you need to stop your ranting on. They've just lost a mate, and you getting all worked up like you always do isn't helping."

I thought she'd scream in outrage at his cheek, but instead her tone dropped to almost a whisper. "Just because you knew me when I was in there," she said, whisking her finger around to point right at me, though I doubt she realized it, "doesn't mean you know me now. It doesn't mean you *ever* knew me."

Alice stepped forward until she was parallel with Trent, but looked past him. "Question your men. Find out who did this. You have twenty-four hours."

She stormed from the barn without looking back. I stared at Trent, knowing I wouldn't get an explanation, but it looked like he wanted to say something. He stared right back at me for a long time before shaking his head and turning to bark orders at his men. Within the hour, the body and most of the guards were gone, and my brothers had stolen my bedding to turn the little alcove into a blanket-and-pillow fort, where they had promptly fallen asleep.

I sat in the middle of the cell floor, eyes closed, trying to focus on the quiet around me for a while just as Trent had taught me to do. He said that learning the normal sounds of any environment would help me to discern when something was different, no matter how subtle.

Evidently, that little trick of his doesn't work well enough to notice a murder happening right beside you in the dark, Pretend Lock said.

Listening wasn't exactly my priority when I was hanging from the barn rafters and being charged by two men.

Or perhaps nothing was different. Pretend Lock was as infuriatingly clever as Actual Lock. And he was right.

Perhaps the reason we hadn't noticed was that nothing was different, or, to be more specific, no *one* was different. If no one unexpected had entered the barn—if it had been an inside job . . . My eyes blinked open at the thought, only to find Trent sitting outside the bars, watching me.

"What did you learn?" he asked.

"That I'm possibly going mad in this place." I toyed with the idea of telling him that he might have a murderer on his staff, but I wasn't sure fueling Alice's paranoia would be to my advantage.

Trent studied my face for a moment, then let go of whatever question I thought he was going to ask me.

"Would it concern you to know that I'm starting to hear voices in my head?" Not exactly true. It was only the one voice.

Trent waved off my completely valid concerns, but he didn't leave.

After a few seconds I asked, "She's actually leaving the boys here? Without a chaperone?"

"She thinks they'll be safer in there with you."

"She's right. Though we could all be safer if you'd open the door and let us go."

Trent grunted his agreement, though he made no move to act. Of course he didn't. I still hadn't discovered what Alice had on him, much less how to free him from the hold she had over him. I hadn't even figured out whether or not he'd help us at all.

"What is she afraid of?" I asked.

Trent didn't answer.

"Why safer in here?"

"Someone killed a man right next to us while we fought. Doesn't that frighten you at all?"

"Are *you* frightened?"

Trent studied my face, then shook his head. "I sometimes forget what you are."

He walked away before I could think of how to answer that, leaving me in my cage for the night. A cold draft filtered through the bars, and then the barn doors shut, and the lock clanked as it fell into place—my nightly reminder of my predicament. I could escape Trent. I could beat him. But none of that granted me my freedom. The barn was still my prison and Alice my warden—until she slipped up, that is.

And I was very sure she'd slip up eventually. She wouldn't be able to hold me forever.

In fact, it took Alice exactly seven more days to screw up. Three to make her first mistake, and it all started with her shouting entrance into the barn.

"There'll be no missteps tonight, gentlemen! Don't forget what's at stake here."

I heard Lucas's voice, but I couldn't make out what he was saying or how Alice responded, even when I stood as close to them as my cell would allow. But I did hear her say something like, "You'll get your payment in full at the end of the week." I mightn't have learned anything else, but Alice couldn't help but come over to comment on my continued imprisonment.

"You're being quiet. Should I be concerned?"

"When I come for you, it won't be quiet."

Alice chuckled. "Still acting out? And here I am about to give you a present."

"Letting me go?"

She laughed again. "Better! I'm sending your brothers to stay the night with you."

The second time in three days, and the last time she'd sent them to me to keep them safe. I had to know what was going on. I moved closer to the bars to study her expression when I asked, "Why?"

"Must I have a reason?" She was too good at masking herself in careless amusement for me to see anything useful. But I supposed knowing it was only a mask was something.

"Yes. You always have a reason for everything."

"I'm having a visitor, and I want the house to myself."

She spoke in this flirty way that was supposed to make me think she was going on a date, but I didn't buy it. I suspected the first half of what she said was true, but she shifted her eyes away when she said the second half. "Maybe if you tell me what's really going on, I can help."

She seemed to consider that. "*Would* you help me?"

"I'd help my brothers."

Alice stepped closer, but not near enough so I could reach her. She was very careful about that. "If you really cared for your brothers as much as you say you do, you'd join me. You'll never find anyone who loves them more than me."

I entertained an image of me pulling Alice up against the bars and explaining that I would never leave my brothers' care to a manipulative, psychopathic bitch like her. But until we escaped, she had power over them, over how often I got to see them, and I couldn't risk making her too angry. Not yet.

"When will my brothers be here?"

"Soon," Alice said, donning her most chipper facade. "Think about what I said."

Had I wounded her? Perhaps I had. But did she really think she could convince someone to follow her by locking them up in a prison cell? Was that what had happened to her?

Chapter 6

This time when the boys arrived, Nurse Olivia was ushering them inside my cage. She bowed her head to me in some kind of formal greeting, and I tried my best not to laugh at that. Over the last few months, I'd learned that Liv, as she wanted me to call her, had grown up in Piddinghoe and used to spend her summers on the farm, circling in orbit around the five-years-older Alice as if she were a mysterious American sun.

The mystique of Alice had lingered throughout the years, increasing when she would be gone for longer and longer periods, coming home with a variety of new friends, hair colors, and hush-hush identities. Which was how Liv had met my mum. She'd known me as well from way back then, though I was too young to remember. Still, we'd become fast friends, and it had been especially entertaining to watch her loyalties shift from Alice to me as she became more and more appalled at my "auntie's" behavior.

From the moment she'd agreed to help me escape, she'd put on a show for Alice—all formalities and professionalism—a facade that quickly faded whenever we were alone.

"She's not here," I said over the noise of my brothers trying to decide where best to set up their sleeping bags. "Though she told me the boys would be coming. Just not why."

Liv nodded. "Something's happened, but I couldn't figure out what before she sent us here. I did manage to bring this."

We sat on the cot, and she glanced around to check for spying eyes before passing me a brochure. I double-checked that Lucas still had his back to us, then arranged a blanket on my lap so I could open the booklet under the cover.

The Whittington International Academy was a boys-only boarding school in the States. Despite its posh name, the school itself seemed to mix high academics with actual playtime and lots of focus on the arts. There was even a special-needs program for Michael and a garden the kids could work in if they wanted.

"Michael's healthy enough to travel?"

Liv nodded.

I'd looked at a dozen of these brochures that Liv had snuck in to me either herself or through the boys. I'd looked at this one several times before, but this time the pictures sent a pang through my chest, because the boys' acceptance letter to the school was tucked inside. "Only a few weeks," I whispered. "We'll only be apart for a little while."

Liv rested her hand on my shoulder in that way she had that was somehow reassuring and warm, but nonintrusive. "You're doing what's best for them. You're removing them from an impossible situation and keeping them safe." She paused, but I could feel the unspoken question that lingered in the air.

"I can't go with them," I said. "I have to make sure no one comes looking for them ever again. I have to make it safe."

Liv nodded and sat up a little straighter. "Payment has been sent. Their acceptance is secured."

"You found the money, then?"

"It was right where you said."

I smiled at that and said a silent thank-you to Alice, our unknowing benefactor. Liv was one of the few people allowed to come and go from the farm as she pleased, which meant she was also the perfect person to clear out the cash from Alice and my mum's hiding spot by St. John's Church.

"I took exactly half like you said. There may be more there than you think."

"More?"

"Much more than you said would be there. I saw the stack you told me about, with the plastic wrapped around it. But there was another stack on top and a third to the side. And there were gold coins and jewelry in a sack."

"Of course." It was all so clear the moment she described it. Obviously Alice had consolidated her wealth in the best hiding place she knew. "She's getting ready to leave. I should have known."

"I took the entire stack and half of another. I left the gold and jewels alone, though. Did I take too much?"

"No. And you can have as much of our half as you'd like. I only need to set up the boys and put some away for when I can join them. Just to get us started."

"It's too much."

"You're saving our lives. I'm trusting you with theirs. The very least I can give you is money."

"I've taken enough to live quite nicely for a year in the States, and set aside plenty for when you come to relieve me. The rest I'll take to my cousin. He said he can put it into a trust for you and the boys in London. You can transfer funds as you need overseas within what the law will allow."

"You've paid him as well, for all the legal advice?"

Liv nodded and started to smile, but paused a moment to study my face, like it was the last time she'd ever see it. "I wasn't sure, you know. That night when you attacked Miss Alice the way you did. I thought maybe those boys had no one in the world to care for them. I'm glad I was wrong."

I closed the brochure and reluctantly passed it back to Liv. "I think I heard her say we're leaving for America at the end of the week."

"Very well. I'll have the boys' things packed and ready."

"Four days," I said. "Four days to figure out how to escape clean and give you a head start."

"Are you sure you want to do it this way? It might be easier to run away once we're all in America. She wouldn't know where to find us."

I shook my head. "Alice and I have business to attend to here. Neither of us are crossing that ocean. I have to come up with a way that lets you leave without us. "

"Couldn't you use the extra money to pay off the guards?"

"I could try, but I don't know how much Alice has promised them, and Trent isn't in it for the money. . . ."

Saying his name evoked the memory of my begging him to help that night in the garden and his refusal. He'd said she promised the guards double their pay if they got all of us on the plane to America. I knew then that they'd never get those bonuses, because I wasn't getting on that plane. But what if she *couldn't* pay?

I stared at Liv. "I need you to go back and take all the money. All of it. The jewels and gold, too. There can't be a note left in that hiding space."

"Why?"

I grinned. "I think I've figured out the first half of my escape plan."

The barn door opened, and Liv stood quickly, pretending to check on my brothers. Alice walked in, the very picture of poise. She was even dolled up as though she were going on an actual date. For the slimmest of seconds, I almost believed her story, but I knew it couldn't be true.

"You'll be glad to know that I'm planning to free you of this cage soon."

"Are you sure I'm all fixed the way you'd like? I understand it took the last girl in this cage more than two hundred twenty-three days."

Alice glanced from Liv to me.

"Oh, sorry. Did you not want her to know?" I stepped toward the bars and stage-whispered, "Was it Mummy or Daddy who kept you in here? Were they doing it for your own good?"

Alice smirked and whispered back. "Did you ever consider

that it was all a farce? That I marked up that door on the off chance that there was enough humanity left in you to feel pity for me?"

I smiled. "Pity for my captor?"

Alice didn't smile. "For your protector. For your guardian. For your friend."

The audacity of her words sent heat through my chest. "My *friend*?"

"I'd like to be." She'd tried this tactic with me before, but this time she actually seemed earnest. Desperate. Something definitely had changed.

I gestured around me. "Is this how you treat your friends?"

"I wouldn't have to if you'd drop the attitude and realize how much I've done for you. We're about to leave for a strange country. You're going to need as many friends as you can get."

"My last friend was left strangled under a tree. Are you sure you want to make that offer?"

"That wasn't your fault."

"No. But what did you call it? My sin?"

Alice's look of sincerity dropped to nothing.

I tilted my head and studied her face before I said, "Do you really think I want to be friends with someone like you?"

She recovered from my barb quickly, but not fast enough to make me think it had all been a ploy. "Then maybe we'll leave you behind."

I didn't react to the threat. I couldn't allow myself to show my true fear at her words. But she knew.

"No witty comeback? Does that mean you're ready to play nice?"

I didn't say anything, and I didn't look away. But my insides felt like they were boiling.

"Don't forget that I'm their aunt now. I'm their *legal* guardian, so unless you're ready to follow through on all your threats, we're stuck with each other from now on. You'll get used to the idea eventually." She studied my face. "Or not. Either way, you'll follow me until one of us dies."

I forced a grin, which was apparently not the reaction Alice expected. "Be careful what you wish for, Auntie."

Chapter 7

My brothers fell asleep rather readily, leaving me awake with three posted guards that night. They prowled the barn and did random checks for my location. If I didn't respond, every corner of the cell would be lit up with flashlights. I thought at first that I'd just pissed Alice off, but then I remembered about her "date."

And that we were leaving soon.

And what she'd said a few days ago: *Do you think this is a coincidence? Now, of all times?*

She was worried because she was planning something. It was the only possibility that made sense. And tonight she was meeting with someone important. I had to find out who it was, which meant I had to be believably asleep the next time the guards checked.

I quickly tiptoed my way through the maze of my brothers' sleeping bags and to my cot, then assumed the most careless sleep position I could think of. I waited, and to distract myself, I thought through what I knew already and tried to decipher Alice's plans.

Alice wanted to be my mum, I knew that for sure. Only not the Emily Moriarty I'd known. She wanted to be Emily Ferris, the woman my mum was before she'd met my father. She wanted to be a mastermind, and to pull jobs, she wanted me on her team. But I didn't know what she wanted me to do. Not really. She thought she could control me with access to my brothers, but she had to know by now that I would always be looking for a way to escape her, to destroy her plans. Did she really think she could use me as . . . what had Trent called me? Her sword?

No. But what, then? What would a con artist want with an underage, hostile student who hadn't even taken her A levels yet?

I was interrupted from my thoughts by the sweep of light across my face. I groaned and turned over in what I hoped was a believably sleepy way.

I saw the light flash around me and then heard a hoarse whisper. "Oy! You awake in there?" I focused on regulating my breathing, exhaling just enough to make my inhales seem as natural as possible. Lucas—I was pretty sure it was Lucas—called out quietly twice more within the next half hour, and when I didn't stir, he gave up and the light went away.

"Sleeping. Which of you's going out? They'll need an extra at the gate."

I didn't wait to hear who it'd be. I was up and moving while Lucas was still walking away from my cell, and used the alcove escape route to climb up in the rafters before he turned off his flashlight. And then it was completely dark. I grinned.

Four months ago, I'd have been frozen on a single wobbling rafter, afraid to move. But Trent had taught me well. I gave my eyes a few seconds to adjust, then moved toward the center support beam to make sure none of the rafters squeaked under my steps.

It felt like a marathon of careful movements before I could climb back down. I dropped into the dirt right by the barn door, pulled my hands into my sleeves, and pulled my hair down over my face to wait in the dark corner for the guard to leave. I held the door before it could shut behind him, then slipped out, timing my steps with his gait so he wouldn't hear me. From there I worked my way to the garden. There were more guards than usual, roaming the grounds, which only made me more suspicious.

Almost ten minutes passed before I spotted a gap in their shifting pattern of walking the property—one that hadn't been there when I first hid among the vegetables in the garden. I didn't take the time to think too much of it, but I was careful when I rounded the house. I ducked below windows and stayed out of the glow that emanated from them. But I didn't stray too far, and when I came to the other side of the kitchen area, I heard voices. They were faint at first but steady. I passed some kind of mudroom that extended off the house and then ducked under a frosted window, most likely the restroom. The voices got louder. Loud enough to hear if I stood just to the side of the big bay window that gave me a view into the sitting room.

"And who will pay our expenses to the States?" asked a

man. His voice was deep and tonal, like the lowest voice in a barbershop quartet.

Alice spoke next. "Your expenses will be covered, but only for travel. We'll plan a job within the first month, however, so money shouldn't be a problem."

"I'll need some papers to fool my mom." This voice I thought I recognized, but it was impossible. So I moved closer to the window and closed my eyes to focus my hearing. It just couldn't be her.

"Something along the lines of a school trip?"

"That'll work. Make it something I won with my grades, and she'll force me to go." Lily. It was Lily Patel, here in Piddinghoe. And she was planning to go with Alice to the States?

I peeked around the frame of the window, still in disbelief, but there she was, sitting on some kind of stool near the hearth. There were maybe four or five others—at least three men and another woman—but I studied her, as if she were an Imaginary like Lock, thinking that if I looked at her long enough, she'd fade away like he always had. But she stayed there in Alice's sitting room, as real as all the others. I could even see the black ribbon holding her father's cross pendant disappearing under her collar and a brand-new handbag leaning up against her crossed ankles.

Of course it was Lily. She wanted so much to revive Sorte Juntos. She was desperate to keep a connection to her father through some ridiculous idea of legacy. And Alice had been the one with the burner phone that night in the park, spying on Lily during her drunken rantings against her mother. Alice had seen it all and had made Lily her mark.

I closed my eyes, wondering just how deep Alice had her hooks into Lily and berating myself for how slow I'd been to see it. And when I opened them, I was staring right into Lily's eyes.

I shrank back into the shadows, but it was too late. I knew she'd seen me and could so easily point me out, without ever knowing the mess she was throwing me into. So I stayed still for a few seconds, and when it didn't seem like any kind of alarm had been raised, I peered back through the window. Lily only gave me a side glance this time, and she kept her head mostly facing forward so Alice and the others wouldn't notice.

She was way more clever than I gave her credit for, which she proved again when she dropped her hand down by her side and started to form letters with her fingers. First an *L*, then an *O*, then another *O*. I waited for another side glance and then nodded and snuck back toward the frosted-glass window.

A sound somewhere up ahead made me retreat away from the house into a nearby hedge. I watched as a figure in black walked by, taking almost my exact path along the house. He seemed familiar, but it wasn't until he reached the bathroom window that he faced me. And then the window opened, letting a brighter light out that shone full on his face.

Stan. He ducked and pressed his shoulders up against the siding of the house to slide by underneath. I waited where I was until he was past the mudroom and heading toward the sitting room window. Part of me wanted to follow him and see what he was doing, but Lily's face had already appeared in the bathroom window. I couldn't have her call my name and alert him that I was there.

I checked to make sure Stan's back was still to me, then ran for the house. At practically the same time, I asked, "How are you here?" and Lily asked, "When did you get here?"

"Me first," Lily said. "When did you get here and why are you hiding outside?"

I shushed her and moved closer before I whispered, "What did Alice tell you about me?"

"She lied. She said you had changed schools to get away from the rumors and gossip. I knew that wasn't true."

"It isn't." I stopped to listen for approaching steps, and when there weren't any, I leaned back against the house.

"Why are you hiding out here? Where have you been?"

I sighed. "I need your help."

When she didn't respond, I said, "I don't have time to tell you everything now, but I'm coming back to London soon. I'm going to take down my father and all his men, but I'll need your help to do it." I glanced up, expecting to see a little bit of glee from her at the prospect of doing anything that would damage my father, but she seemed stoic. "Will you help me?"

She didn't answer right away, and when I looked back, I was surprised to see how dark Lily's expression had grown. "He dies first."

"What?"

"That's my condition. I don't want your father to be taken down. I want him to die, and I want him to die before anything else happens."

"I want him dead more than you do, but it might be easier to get to him if his men are all out of the way."

"No," she said, her voice cracking in what sounded more like pain than anger to me. "Every day that he breathes is a day he stole from my father and I can't have that. Not one more day. I can't bear it."

I didn't know what to say to that, so I kept quiet and looked away to let her dry her tears in private, but I could hear them in her voice.

"He dies first and I'll help you in any way you want."

I nodded my promise and, for just a moment, wondered at how small it felt to make such a giant vow. I'd just promised to kill my own father the way some might agree to meet up for ice cream after class. It was such a certainty to me that he would die. In my mind, he was already dead. It was just the chore of actually killing him that was still left to do. And I would do it with every pleasure.

"You can help me first with information," I said. But then we both heard voices growing louder, coming down the hall, and I kept quiet until they passed. "Quickly, tell me what she's planning."

Lily smiled widely. "It's brilliant. She's taking Sorte Juntos to America. We'll be there for three months, and I'll be the locksmith just like my dad."

"And you're leaving soon?"

"She leaves in four days and I'm to join them in a month."

I frowned.

"But you know all this, Mori. You're supposed to be part of it."

I shook my head. "I'm not. She's only keeping me here by using my brothers as leverage."

"Alice? But she's your aunt."

"I don't have time to explain. But you shouldn't make any plans, Lily. If I'm to escape, I'll have to stop her from leaving as well, which means . . ."

Her smile dropped. "No Sorte Juntos in America."

"It can't be helped."

She sighed. "It's the only way?"

I nodded. "If she takes me with her to America, I'll never be able to reach my father. It has to be now."

"Priorities," she said.

I heard faint footsteps in the dark and thought Stan might be coming back. "I have to go. I'll find you as soon as I reach London."

"Right. And you owe me a bank heist."

I grinned. "We'll have to see about that."

Chapter 8

I made it back to the garden with ease. Alice's new team members were leaving the farm, and half the guards were leaving with them. I knew this was the ideal time to go back to my cell. I had this perfect window to sneak in when I was almost guaranteed a clear path. I could make it back to my cot with no one knowing I'd left. And my brothers were there. I could wake them to play midnight games . . . just in case.

Just in case? Pretend Lock asked.

I tried to ignore him, but, as in reality, my Lock was never one to mind someone else's feelings about anything.

In case your plans go wrong? In case you can't find a way to get them away from her?

I felt a shiver run through me and turned my head away, so he couldn't see my expression. But it didn't help. He was sitting in front of me no matter where I looked.

In case your only way to escape is to leave them behind?

"No."

I hadn't meant to say the word aloud, nor had I meant a silly re-creation of Sherlock Holmes to bring me to tears, but when I opened my eyes again, I couldn't see him through the blur. And when I blinked, he was gone. Pretend Lock never stayed to pick up the pieces. Even in my weakened state of barn-induced madness, I couldn't allow myself to be comforted by my own delusion.

Or maybe I was stalling, still unwilling to give up my freedom for the chance to play hangman or noughts and crosses by flashlight in the dirt of my cell. The idea of willingly putting myself back into that horrible, mind-deadening space was more than I could bear. Not yet. My thoughts were too large to fit in that building. They screamed inside my head in a constant refrain, despite how hard I tried to push them down. I played games to quash my thoughts. I repeated silly quotes from silly authors who spent their days making up silly stories when they could have been doing something real, something important.

Sadie would've stopped being my friend if she'd ever heard me say that.

Sadie. God, how I wished I could stop thinking about Sadie. Stop seeing her wide eyes in that drawing and my father's hand around her throat.

I'd thought promising to kill my father was small—a nothing. That was easy to think when I was making promises to Lily, but it was so large in my mind every day. He was large, his death was large, and perhaps my true reasons to end his life should have been just as large. But they weren't.

What are your reasons? Imaginary Lock was back, sitting among the aubergines, their deep purple a fitting color for his dirt throne. He was reading a book, and couldn't even bother to look up from the text to get my answer.

Not that the answer was particularly compelling. When I thought of all the reasons why my father should die, I could only think of Sadie, who brought a pie, and my brothers, who knew every hiding place in our home to escape him, and Lily's father, who drank beer from black cans—all of them resided in a constant spinning mass within a jar labeled REASONS in my mind.

Imaginary Lock looked up from his book. *A pie. A can of beer. Those are your real reasons?*

No, I answered him. *But they are enough.*

The last set of car taillights disappeared down the road outside the farm, and I watched Alice stride through the grass back to her house with a giant smile that I wanted to claw from her mouth.

Will you kill her as well? Lock asked, turning the page of his book.

A fair question. I'd let myself trust Alice. I thought surely we'd found the one person in all the earth who wouldn't lay a finger on us. I trusted her with the only people who meant anything to me. . . .

Except for Sherlock. I closed my eyes to make him go away, and when I opened them, his aubergine throne was empty. But that didn't chase him from my thoughts. No matter how I tried, nothing I did could get him out of my head, and I hated him for that. I hated time. Because that was the real culprit. Nearly five months locked in a cage with nothing but time and no distraction.

Alone with my thoughts, I couldn't repel them like I wanted. I couldn't lock them in a room and ignore the knocking, because there was nothing to drown out the sounds. Just me. So I sat among the plants I'd toddled through when I was small, and I closed my eyes and listened to the sounds of the night—the sounds of the farm that used to be my mum's sanctuary.

The ideas of sanctuary and my mum didn't go together well. And that thought felt traitorous, as did almost all thoughts of my mum in this place. I wanted to love her, to remember only the woman who showed me how to flip a coin across my fingers and who ferociously danced aikido katas with her sword. But all that I knew about her was ruined now. Her sword was no longer part of her graceful, dangerous movements; it was a weapon that tore through the flesh of her best friends. Her coin was no longer a childish trinket; it was a symbol of her past crimes. Even that house she bought with the spoils of her heists was tainted—it held memories of the bloodied faces of her children, of an old, battered woman bleeding to death on the carpet.

My mum's secrets even ruined my happiest childhood memory. This farm was supposed to be a safe space—this garden a testament to what real love looked like. She was everywhere here, and there were nights that I could've escaped my prison but didn't because I wasn't ready to face her and all the things she could've done to help us before she died.

She could have brought us all here. She could have taken her money from her stash with Alice and helped us all to escape my father. When she knew she was sick, we could have run. *Why* had she left us there? With him? Why, when she knew who he was?

I knew the answers. Of course I did. I just hadn't wanted to admit them to myself, because I knew I would hate her after. And then even she herself would be ruined. So I pretended that I didn't know she was a monster. That only a monster could be loved by the horror show that was my father. Only a monster loves one in return. She didn't help us escape because she loved him. Or she didn't want to die alone. Did it matter which? We weren't enough for her. She needed him more than she cared about what would happen to us when she was gone.

Or maybe she'd known this farm wasn't the escape I wanted to believe it was. That thought made me feel better. If I could believe my idyllic, pastoral memories of this garden and Alice's parents were just a distraction from the farm's dark underbelly—the darkness that locked Alice in a cage and turned her into a fraud, a thief, and a killer—then I could forgive my mum for not leaving us here. I could sit in that tainted garden and listen to the night in a place that was no one's sanctuary.

But the night didn't wear clothes that rustled. The night didn't breathe. My non-sanctuary had been invaded.

"Did you know her?" I asked the man sitting behind me. It could only be Trent. Any other guard would have sounded the alarm right away. "Did you know my mum?"

"I met her."

"Tell me something bad about her."

"Why would you want that?"

"Because no one ever talks about the bad things after you die, but that doesn't make them go away. Will you tell me something bad about my dead mum?"

"How would I know?"

"Tell me, and I'll tell you something about her that you'll like."

"All right. Your mum was a snob."

I smiled. "There's a story there."

"No story. Alice brought me to the farm so I could audition for Emily's little troupe of thieves."

"I take it she didn't want you."

"She had no use for my skills. That's how she put it. And then she changed the subject and acted like I wasn't in the room."

"And that hurt your feelings?"

He didn't answer me with more than a grunt, but I could practically hear his internal grumbling.

"And now shall I tell you something you'll like? My mum liked to keep secrets from everybody. And Alice? She likes to make empty threats."

"Why would I like that?"

"It means your secrets die with Alice. She doesn't know how to hurt you from beyond the grave. She's all threat, no bite."

"How do you know her threats are empty?"

I glanced around us and stood up. "She's not nearly as clever as she thinks she is."

That made Trent grin. He stood as well. "Why are you telling me all this?"

"Because I'm not going with Alice to America and neither are my brothers."

I could see he didn't believe me, but still he said, "I can't give you my help."

"I'd like to have it. I don't need it."

He studied my face and I stared back. He could believe me or not, but in the end I was leaving with or without him. And if he took her side, he might become a casualty of Alice's hubris. I didn't want that, but I wouldn't let it change my plans, either.

"I'm not sure I'm willing to risk it on your say alone," he said.

I nodded and stared at the front gate of the farm. If I just started to run, how far could I make it before one of them caught up to me? Would I even make it out onto the road? It was a nice fantasy, but Trent placed himself in my way before I could take even a step.

"What are you planning?"

He couldn't have expected an answer to that, so I left him to drown in his silent expectation and turned back toward the barn. I thought he might follow me, or try to force it out of me, but he didn't. In fact, he didn't speak again until I'd reached the doorway of the barn. And then I heard him say, "You can't beat all of us."

I grinned as I snuck inside. He was right, but then, I wouldn't need to.

Chapter 9

After Alice came to fetch my brothers for breakfast the next morning, I didn't see any of them for the next twenty-four hours. It was just long enough to let the doubts creep in, that maybe Alice had let me overhear her timeline on purpose, that maybe they had already left for the States without me. But then Trent came in directing men carrying boxes, and as the towers of Alice's belongings grew higher, I knew that they were still packing. At least for now.

I thought about sneaking out, just to check on the boys and Olivia, to make sure they were packed and ready, to tell them what I had planned. But Trent never seemed to leave the barn anymore. It was like now that he knew I had a plan to escape, he'd decided to keep an eye on me. Sadly for him, my plan involved very little stealth. His presence wasn't going to stop anything.

But I had to have perfect timing.

Which was why I waited to act until days later, when I overheard a guard tell Trent that Alice had left the farm to run an errand. And then I waited about as long as I thought it might take to drive to the churchyard and open the hiding spot where Alice's money was once kept. And right about the time I estimated Alice would be realizing all her money was gone, I walked up behind Lucas and leaned against the bars directly to his left.

"Do you want to know a secret?"

Lucas jumped at the sound of my voice, then glared at me over his shoulder. "Go back to your cot."

"I can, but then you'll fall for Alice's tricks, and I just think it's so unfair."

"What're you on about?"

I leaned in closer to his ear, and he leaned back toward the bars, which goes to show that some men learn nothing from their mistakes. Still, as tempting as it was to yank him back into a chokehold again, I had more important moves to make in today's game. "You aren't getting paid today, because Alice doesn't have any money."

Lucas turned to stare at me. "You're lying."

I shrugged. "Am I? I suppose we'll find out soon enough."

In my periphery, I saw Trent glance our way and start to step toward us, but then another guard came up to him with a question.

Lucas tried to play off what I'd said. But I could see he was riled up on the inside. "You're lying. Why'd you think I'd fall for that?"

"I'll tell you what. If I'm lying, then Alice will come back from her errand with a smile on her face and money in envelopes for each of you. If I'm telling the truth, she'll come back scowling and probably try to blame me for her money being gone."

"Why would she blame you?"

I sighed. "It's one of her oldest tricks. She makes all these promises to the men who follow her, and when it's time to pay, she acts like she was the victim of a theft and tries to turn her men on the supposed thief while she gets away."

"But you've been in this cage. We've all seen you trapped in here. How could she blame you?"

"I know. It makes no sense. But she's always so convincing. It's not like this is the first time she's done it."

Lucas still looked at me with a scrunched-up, skeptical expression that made me think maybe I hadn't convinced him. But almost as soon as I'd wandered back to my cot, he ran over and started whispering to the men who stood by the door. I grinned. My pawn was in play.

After a bit, Lucas came back to stand guard near the gate of my cell. I could tell he was trying to act like nothing had changed, but every time a car drove up, he craned his neck to see who'd come up the drive.

"You starting trouble?" Trent asked, walking up to my cell. His expression was a lot more serious than his tone. If I went by face alone, I'd have thought I was about to be punished.

"I gave you the chance to be on the right side of today."

He wasn't the easiest man to read, but he seemed to exchange his anger for a bit of fear, or maybe I just assumed that was the case when he asked, "What have you done?"

I stared up at the rafters. "What could I possibly do under your perpetual watch?"

"Plenty," was his only reply. And then he stepped away, but not too far, I noticed.

I pulled out my already packed bag and placed it next to the cot for easy access.

Not ten minutes later I heard a car pull up and knew Alice had arrived at the farm. I didn't need to see her to know she was frowning when she entered the barn; I only needed to watch the panic set in on Lucas's face as he realized he wasn't going to be paid. For just a minute I felt a little bad for the men who'd followed Alice. But then I remembered that they'd held a teenage girl prisoner in a horse barn for nearly five months' time.

"WHERE IS IT?!" Alice roared the question as she stomped into the barn.

I pretended to study my nails, which were in desperate need of a manicure. Thankfully, my life in dirt was almost over.

"What have you done with it?"

I looked up with my best surprised expression. "What are you talking about?"

She looked around and lowered her voice, like she'd just realized we had an audience. But it was too late. Almost all the guards had come to the barn for their payday, and all their attention was fully focused on what was about to transpire.

"You know very well what I'm talking about. What have you done with my money?"

"What money?" I asked. "You've never had any money." I

glanced at Lucas with a shrug, which set him off. He immediately ran over to confer with a handful of the other guards.

"You took it! I know you did. You're the only other person who knew where it was."

I stood and slid my hands up to my hips. "And how would I do that? I've been locked in here. *You* locked me in here. How in the world would I ever have access to your money? Stop lying, Aunt Alice. It doesn't suit you."

One of the larger guards rambled toward us. "Oy! Do you really not have the money to pay us?"

Alice narrowed her eyes at me and started stomping for my gate. "Oh, I'll get it. She'll tell me where it is if I have to beat it out of her."

It was perfect, really. I'd thought for a minute that I'd pulled the trigger too soon, and I'd have to crawl out of my prison all on my own. But here was Alice, opening the gate for me, like she was in on the plan. I slung the strap of my bag over my head and across my chest, so that by the time she'd unlocked the gate, I was ready to leave. I only had to stir the pot once more, and then walk out the door to meet Olivia and the boys at the car while all of Alice's men demanded answers of her. But then Alice rushed in and slapped me across the face. The rest of the barn fell silent, but Alice did not.

"You'll tell me now, little girl! Give me my mon—"

I punched her to shut her up, and when she swung to punch me back, I grabbed her arm and twisted it behind her, hiking it up until she cried out in pain. A few of the guards started for the gate, but Lucas held up a hand, stopping them.

I pushed Alice up against the bars and spoke slowly into her ear so she could hear me clearly.

"Later, when you realize how badly you've lost to me, think about how merciful I'm being to you right now by not tearing you apart in front of your men. But I warn you. If you survive today, never, ever come and find me again. I won't be this kind twice."

I pushed off of her and rushed toward the gate, like I was trying to escape her next blow, not that I expected her to do more than stand there, scared of what she'd insisted I become. "Stop trying to blame me for your scheming, Aunt Alice. Just own up to what you did."

The questions started as I reached the opening.

"You never had the money you promised us?"

"Is she telling the truth?"

"No!" Alice cried. "That girl's lying to you. She knew where I kept my stash and somehow—"

Lucas didn't even let her finish, playing his part as if I'd scripted it. "She's done this before! She's been tricking us all along."

Before I could step outside my cell, I was stopped by a blond guard who looked like he could have been Alice's brother. "Look me in the eye. She really never had the money?"

I shrugged. "You all knew what kind of person she was. Did you think she'd suddenly stop conning people just because it was you?"

Alice started screaming her answers back, that she had millions but it was all stolen. That she knew I was somehow involved. That they should demand answers from me. That they needed to stop me before I got away. But they didn't believe her, not with Lucas shouting, "That's exactly what she said you'd say!"

I smiled back at Alice right as I took my first step of freedom, just in time to see her lunging at me. She was on my back before I could react, and then we were both on the ground outside the cell, her fingers twisting into my hair to yank it back. She leaned close to say, "You don't leave until I say—"

And I slammed the back of my head into her nose as hard as I could. It worked to get her off me, but two of her men responded on instinct, rushing toward us. I barely had time to rise from the floor and fix my stance before the first one reached me. I kicked him solidly in the left knee, dropping him to the floor, and then spun toward the blond guard who'd been at the door earlier. He didn't seem interested in getting involved, especially once I grabbed a wooden handle from a box to his right, hoping for a weapon with heft. Sadly, it was only the broken shop-broom handle I'd used in my test with Trent.

It would have to be enough. The second of Alice's men grabbed me before I could spin all the way around, but he couldn't get a proper hold because of my bag, so I was able to shove my broom handle between his legs and up until he was groaning and rolling around on the ground.

"Don't let her leave!" Alice shouted. Her face was a mess of blood and dirt from our scuffle, but she was still kicking and writhing to get free of the three men who had her pinned up against the bars. "Idiots!"

That left the two men I'd dropped to the ground, the two door guards who'd backed off from all the drama, and three others, who were moving toward her, not me. So I started for the barn doors, but there was still one impediment to my escape: Trent, who stood directly in my path.

"I can't let you leave," he said.

I tried skirting around him, but I only made it two steps before Trent's hand was on my arm. I swung around, pulling free as I moved, then shoved him back.

"Don't touch me."

"Where's the money?"

In every plan I'd made to get us off that bloody farm, I'd thought that I might have to fight Trent to get away, but I'd secretly hoped he'd finally come to his senses and at the very least look the other way. I hadn't expected this.

"I thought you weren't in it for the money? Or was that all a lie?"

"Tell me where you put it."

"And what? You'll let me go?"

He started to advance and I ducked under his arm, moving closer to the doors in the process.

"Here's a secret: I don't need to tell you anything to leave here."

We faced one another like we were back in training, ready to block each other's blows. But before either of us could make an attack, Alice screamed and we both turned. I couldn't see her anymore through the crowd of men, but I could hear the soft whining of her pleading and the guards' growling replies growing louder as she denied everything. I'd expected they'd be distracted enough to let me escape—I hadn't thought they'd actually hurt her.

For the smallest of moments I let my mind trail through ideas of how to help her without losing my advantage to escape, but then I saw Trent take a step forward and realized he was going to do that for me. So I took a step back. Trent swung his attention toward me. It was such a pathetic scene, really. The two people who probably hated Alice the most trying to decide whether to come to her rescue.

"You have to stop this," he said.

"I won't."

Alice cried out again and Trent flinched.

I took another step back. "You have a choice. You can stop me or save Alice."

She shouted again, promising to get their money, begging for them not to hurt her. And Trent kept looking between me and the men like he couldn't make up his mind.

"What have you done?" he asked, all concern but no movement.

"This is what I had to do to escape without your help."

I turned away then and started walking for the farm-house. Olivia and the boys were already waiting on the drive, motioning for me to hurry. I reached them just as another air-rending scream erupted from the barn behind us, followed by a loud bang. We all jumped, and I pulled Michael behind me. A gun. I recognized the sound, though I'd only heard it two other times in my life. Not even the corrupted police in my father's group of friends carried guns. But we were in the countryside, where shotguns were considered farming tools. Our escape suddenly felt more perilous.

I waited to make sure that shot hadn't been directed toward us. When I was sure we weren't the target, I turned back to my brothers' worried faces. "Quickly now," I said, and pushed on their shoulders. We all started running toward the gate.

I looked back once, just long enough to see Trent at the door of the barn, with a dark smear across his green jacket. Then I passed a tree that blocked off my line of sight, and thankfully his sight line to us as well. But the smear—had it looked wet? *Blood* was my first thought, but I didn't know what it was, I reminded myself. I couldn't see clearly from where we were. And it didn't matter anymore, because I couldn't let anything stop us from escaping.

An out-of-breath Liv, holding Michael's hand, fell back to jog beside me. "I've got a car waiting at the gate of the next farm to take us to the station."

I smiled and took Michael's other hand. "Well done. Let's move faster now."

Chapter 10

When the hired car dropped us at Eastbourne Station, every-thing felt familiar. Well, half-familiar. I'd done this before, sent my brothers off with a woman whom I thought I could trust, while I stayed behind. Eastbourne even had a window panel ceiling, though nothing as grand as London's Victoria Station. My brothers still seemed scared. Freddie was mad at me for not going with them; Seanie was just angry. Only Michael smiled, but that was hardly a comfort.

I helped Olivia settle the boys into the frontmost compart-ment of the train and then stood in the aisle, staring at them. My train didn't leave for another hour, but these boys—I wouldn't see them for weeks. Maybe months. I missed them already.

"These are your papers," Olivia said, pointing to the manila envelope that was poking out of the bag of money and other necessities she'd gathered for me. "Passport under your new name, American dollars and Icelandic króna for your trip."

I was distracted when I said, "Yes, thank you." And then I was a bit heartsick when I crouched down to face my brothers.

"Be good for Olivia. I'll be there as soon as I can. I promise you'll love the new school."

"And if we don't?" asked Seanie.

I rested a hand over his. "If you don't, then I'll give you a twenty-minute sweetshop shopping spree."

Michael started to clap and Seanie smiled widely even after I ruffled his hair. "I'm sure I hate it already," Sean said.

Michael and Sean started talking feverishly about what they'd buy at the shop and how much they could gather in twenty minutes. Freddie leaned forward to speak quietly just to me.

"You shouldn't have said that." He looked down at the floor. "Now he'll be determined to hate it no matter what."

"I'm counting on you, Fred. I need you to keep everyone safe in America."

"Until you get there? You really are coming?"

I drew a cross over my heart. "I promise."

He hugged me and I patted his back until he was ready to let go. And when I stood, I had to blink the tears from my eyes to look at Olivia properly.

She rested a reassuring hand on my shoulder. "I'll take care of them like they are my own family."

I nodded. I didn't know why I trusted her. I shouldn't have with my track record. But I suppose her chosen profession made her seem more trustworthy. Or perhaps it was how readily she admitted that she hadn't trusted me to care for the boys when she'd seen me so out of control. I might have been making a giant mistake all over again, but right then

I felt more assured than I ever had. She was an outsider, a normal person. She was separate from all the criminals in our lives. And she was going to take the boys to a boarding school where I could call and check in on how they were doing. It was going to be all right.

Except for how I'd miss them. And how lost I felt when she let her hand fall from my shoulder. So I took her hand in mine and looked at her. I couldn't speak, so I squeezed her hand and then left the train.

I stood on the platform, watching them and waving until I was staring at empty tracks. I probably stood there too long, or at least that was what I told myself. I also told myself that it wouldn't do to wallow in emotions when I had so much thinking to do, so many plans to make. What I needed was a good distraction, so I looked across at the people waiting along the platform and started to run their demographics in my head.

But right as I'd settled on my list of outliers, including an ornately garbed grandmother clinging to the hand of a young child, my eyes were drawn to the man who stepped up next to them. I almost didn't recognize Stan out of the black clothing that had become a uniform of sorts for my guards at the farm. He looked different in street clothes and with a cap on his head, but I'd spent months staring at his ugly face and listening to his jeers. I'd probably carry his face in my memory for the rest of my life.

I didn't want him to see me, so I moved back just enough to hide myself among the people and still have a good view of him. He seemed to be hiding as well, though I couldn't understand why. He kept glancing up and pulling his cap down lower to conceal his face, so I followed his gaze to the CCTV cameras set to capture a picture of the entire platform. But those are only seen by operators and police.

I leaned back as he turned my way, and when I dared to look again, he was staring at the ground.

Somewhere in the back of my mind I heard the gunshot in the barn, but that couldn't have been Stan. For him to be in the station right in that moment meant he'd left either before or very near when I did. And when I thought about it, I hadn't seen his face in the crowd of guards that surrounded Alice to demand their money. I couldn't remember seeing him that entire morning. I didn't know anything at all about his circumstances, but it seemed odd that he'd have left the farm without even fighting to get paid.

Still, I stayed out of his sight line and kept him in mine. Whether he was trying to find me for Alice or had some other plan in mind, I couldn't let him follow me back to London. I'd reenter my city on my terms, not his. And no one could know I was there. Not yet.

The smell of home is a powerful thing. Even through the hot, dusty smell of the Tube station the minute I stepped off the train, I could tell I was home. And by the time I made it to my beloved Baker Street, I wanted nothing more than to go to the park. My park. And I justified going by creating an errand for myself once I got there. I was tempted to torture myself with a stop at the bandstand, to spend an hour under the branches of the giant willow tree by the lake to make up for five months without paying my penance to Sadie.

But instead I walked straight to the old, two-tiered fountain that had been turned into a planter. I sat on a nearby bench to wait for dusk, and for the paths around the planter to become deserted. Then I placed my hand on the plaque depicting the Tree of Life and tipped it up. Once it clicked, I heard the soft ticks of a timer and ran around to the other side before they stopped. I twisted the clover plaque to the left until the chamber inside was revealed. It seemed somehow poetic and yet still practical to stash my getaway papers and money there. And after waiting for a pair of dog walkers to pass me by, I opened the chamber again and stuffed about two thousand in pound notes on top—just in case.

Then I sat back on the bench, and when the sun had disappeared completely, I pulled out a burner phone and called Lily Patel. I was sure she wouldn't answer a number she didn't recognize, and, as predicted, she let it go to voice mail.

"I'm in London. Meet me tomorrow after school at your dad's place. I'll have a list."

It was completely dark when I walked up Gloucester, looking to rent a room for the night. I found one soon enough, not too posh, and it had a café downstairs where I could take my breakfast in the morning. I needed an early start. It was time to find out all that my father had been up to in the months of his unearned freedom.

Chapter 11

I spent most of the morning hiding across from my
house—and watching. In my confinement, I'd imagined
my father leaving the house early in the morning to start
his day of corruption, with him and his cronies terrorizing
the Westminster Borough of London. I'd imagined myself
following him and finding a way to foil his plans from the
shadows, never revealing it was me who was slowly ruining
him. Then I'd finally lure him into a trap of my choosing,
where I would out myself as his nemesis and take care of
him for good.

What I hadn't imagined was that my father would spend
his first three hours of the day sitting at the kitchen table and
drinking like he always had. Jail hadn't changed him at all; it
had only cost him his job. Honestly, I didn't need to hide. The
whole of London could have pulled up a chair outside the
kitchen windows and watched him stare into space or scroll
through random websites on a tablet he couldn't even bother
to hold upright to read. How pathetically docile the monster
looked, blinking his eyes to clear his stupor enough so he

could stumble his way to the bathroom or collapse on his bed or some other mundane thing.

Was this the man I'd spent my nights plotting against? Was he even worthy of my plans? Would anyone notice if I wandered into the house, pulled a carving knife from the drawer, and plunged it into his chest while he slept?

It was very nearly noon when I caught my reflection in a decidedly empty kitchen window. I'd chosen the wrong way to suss him out. I started back down the street, returning the way I'd come, when I recognized someone from the neighborhood that I knew. Well, "knew" was probably an overstatement, but I was sure she'd recognize me, so I crossed the street and found myself walking right toward 221 Baker Street.

The moment I saw his doorway, I wanted to go inside. My heart even started to race in that way it does when I'm about to do something shocking or stupid or forbidden. And a visit to Sherlock this early in my reconnaissance would be all three, as well as burdensome, as I didn't suppose Lock would let me be off on my own if he knew I were in London.

Or perhaps he would.

It had been nearly five months, and the last Lock knew, I'd refused his invitation to meet him in the park. Five months, and I was sure that he'd returned to his studies and his experiments. Did I really think I'd stroll in, greet him over afternoon tea, and he'd ask me to sit for a catch-up session? Did I expect he'd be thrilled to finally discover my intrusion back into his life? He probably never thought about me at all anymore.

Still, I wanted to go inside—and I could be in and out before anyone knew I was there. I watched for a few minutes, thinking about how I'd break in, or whether I could pick the lock quickly enough to keep from looking suspicious, and quietly enough not to alert anyone who might be in the house. But as I walked toward the steps leading up to his front door, I saw it—the fake rock that held their extra key. That was all the invitation I needed.

I knew exactly how the house would look inside, and still the sameness of it surprised me. It also made me angry. I'd told myself over and over that I wanted Sherlock to go on with his life without me. There was no reason at all for me to be mad now that I knew he had done so. And still, when I found mugs for tea in the sink and a film-wrapped plate half filled with sandwiches in the refrigerator, I scowled.

I'd had all these ideas on how I would show myself to Lock again. On how he would react. How I'd refuse to explain to him what had happened to me until he promised to meet me later. Or maybe I'd never tell him at all, knowing his convoluted imaginings of how I'd spent all those months would be way more intriguing than my slow trip to madness from inside a horse-stall jail cell. But when it was real, when I heard two voices at the front door, instead of posing with a false disinterest in his sitting room, I ran up the stairs to hide.

"And I couldn't for the life of me figure out how you'd known exactly who was lying and where she'd hidden the money." The voice was familiar, but I couldn't seem to place it without taking a peek. "It was an impressive deduction."

I'd almost forgotten his name—Lily's boy. I kept wanting to call him Watkins, but I knew that was wrong. And me with the eidetic memory. I really *had* lost my mind on that farm.

"For the life of you," Lock echoed.

God, he sounded smug. I smiled.

"Would you like to stay for tea? I have sandwiches."

Lily's boy paused. And finally his name jumped out from my memories.

"Watson," I whispered aloud, then covered my mouth and moved back from the top of the stairs and into Lock's room, though I did keep the door cracked open so I could hear what they were saying.

Watson didn't answer right away, which definitely meant he didn't want to stay, but it took him far too long to spit out, "Just came for the book, if that's okay?"

"No, you didn't," Sherlock said in perhaps the most irritatingly arrogant way possible. "But I'll be right back with it."

And really, it was a wonder Watson didn't roll his eyes and storm from the place when Sherlock spoke. It had taken all of five months for Lock to become a torrential storm of jackassery in my absence. I felt like I should apologize to the entire city on his behalf. As it turned out, I'd have to apologize to all of London's citizens save one: John Watson.

"Maybe . . . ," Watson said, after I'd heard Sherlock run up a few steps. "Maybe we could have our tea out. My treat. To thank you for the book?"

I didn't hear Lock respond, but I did hear him start to climb the steps again. I quietly closed his door, which was when I saw it—the string map on the wall, just like it had been so many months ago. Only this map wasn't a web of my father's crimes. This map was about me.

My name was at the center. And something about the way my simple nickname was written in Lock's hand made me freeze in place. He was coming up the stairs. He was most likely coming into his room, but I couldn't look away from all the pins he'd used to mark possible places I'd been. Blue for places he wanted to check, red for places he had? It appeared so. The red pins all had little collars of string, as though their connection to my name had been severed the moment the investigation came up empty. There were only three blue pins left.

The floorboards creaked at the top of the stairs and I ran for the far side of his wardrobe, tucking myself into the corner between it and the wall just as the doorknob started to move. And then he came in, and I wasn't prepared for how it would feel to be in the same room with him.

Idiotically, my first instinct was to jump out of my hiding place. I caught myself literally hanging on to the wardrobe to stop my legs from doing such a thing against my will, as though he were this giant magnet and my core was straining against the pull of him. When he came closer to inspect his bookshelves, my hand wanted so badly to reach out and rest on his arm. Just to touch him, I thought, to let him know I was there. That his search was over. That I was standing right next to him.

Sherlock grabbed a book off his shelf and turned his back

to me, then stopped cold in the center of his room. I thought maybe I'd somehow revealed myself, so I tipped my head to see what he was up to, but he stood very still, book in hand. His head turned just enough to stare at his own bed. He breathed in deeply and then furrowed his brow. He lifted the book to his nose and breathed deeply again. Then he dropped the book back to his side and walked to the door. I thought at first he'd leave, but instead he reached up to rest his hand on the center of his map, just beneath my name.

"Did you once hold this book?" he asked. "Did I stir up the dust that held your perfume just now?"

An ache started pulsing at the center of my chest with his words. I somehow managed to keep silent until he left the room, though I couldn't say how. I felt like someone had turned me inside out. Like everything I knew before I stepped into his room was gone and I had to start over again. Only I couldn't, because I was already changed. It didn't matter that he wasn't.

When I heard the front door close downstairs, I emerged from my hiding place and walked a straight line to his bedroom door. I rested my hand where his had been, just below my name. I'd created a pretend version of Lock, knowing how mad that made me seem. How long, I wondered, had he been speaking to my name on this bloody map?

I made a fist with my hand and let my gaze wander down to the final three blue pins. I huffed out a breath when I found the one that connected my name to Piddinghoe.

He would have found me, my Lock. Maybe it would have

taken him weeks or another month, but he would have found me. And maybe then everything would've been different. Wouldn't it?

"Too late," I whispered.

With Lock to help me, I could have found a way past Alice and her guards without anyone getting hurt. Without having to hear Alice's screams or the echoing crack of a gunshot.

"Too late," I growled through clenched teeth, then started pulling pins from their places and tearing cards and papers and receipts down onto the floor.

I was breathing heavily when I was done, like a madwoman after a tantrum. Only then did it occur to me that the mess I'd made would be a message I didn't particularly want to send. So I knelt down on his rug and made a quaint little pile of pins. I stacked the pages and cards up nicely right next to it and bundled the strings.

When everything was ordered, I stood, but the sparkle of a pin hidden near his bed got my attention. As did the floral pattern on the cardboard box the pin was resting against. *The box*.

I pulled it out from under the bed quickly and knocked the lid off. And right in the center was a frame with little orange Xs across the broken glass.

My mum's things. Had they been here in his room all this time? I couldn't believe I'd forgotten this box for so long. And then I couldn't believe he'd kept it there under his bed. A secret. Had he kept these things for me? Or from me? I would never know, which meant it didn't really matter. It only mattered that they were mine.

I left that day with my box of things. I made sure I was gone before he returned, though he'd know I'd been there. He'd have to know now that I'd destroyed his work. I grinned a bit at the thought of how Lock would put it all together, the pieces of his map piled next to his bed, all except for the one red pin pushed through the center of the first letter of my name to hold it against his pillow. Would he notice right away that my mum's things were missing? Would he wonder where I was?

He'd know soon enough. And it would be better this way. The next time he'd see me would be out on the street, where neither of us would have the space or silence to say anything we'd regret later. Next time, all of London would be watching.

Chapter 12

I dropped the box at my hotel room and grabbed a cap and hoodie on my way out. I couldn't let myself be recognized by any of our neighbors. I couldn't risk that they might tell my dad they'd seen me.

Lily beat me to the clearing in Regent's Park. She'd laid out a blanket and was staring at the tree where her father was murdered. No beer or flowers this time. Evidently, five months was enough time to get over her ritual.

Without turning to face me, she said, "I'm ready to hear your explanation."

"Explanation for what?"

"You said you'd explain later, why you were at Alice's countryside house."

"And here I thought you wanted my father dead as soon as possible."

Lily didn't answer, leaving me to wrestle with her quiet expectation. But I wasn't really sure how much I wanted to tell her beyond what she already knew. So I moved closer to her blanket and sat down between her and the tree. I thought for sure seeing me would break her silence, but it didn't. Instead, she stared at me, which made everything worse. So I decided to frame my story around the one thing I knew she cared about.

"When I heard my father was going to be released on court bail, I packed us all up to go to America to hide my brothers from him. But at the last minute I stayed behind, because I knew he needed to die."

I glanced up at Lily, and her expression was this beautiful mix of anger and pleasure at my words. I'd seen that expression so often in the mirror. That Lily didn't even bother to mask her feelings told me two things—she was far more brutal than I'd ever expected, and I had her. She was one of my people now. I looked back down at the stitching across the blanket and decided to slice through the binds that Alice had managed to wrap around Lily as well. That would be easy enough.

"Alice wanted me to forget about my dad and be part of her Sorte Juntos team in America, but she knew I would refuse until I knew my dad was dead. So she had me kidnapped in London and imprisoned me in a cage in her horse barn."

"That's where you were?"

I nodded.

Lily seemed to consider that, then asked, "But if you could escape the cage like you did that night, why didn't you just run away?"

"My brothers were there as well. I couldn't leave without them."

Lily frowned. "You should have just agreed to be on the crew."

"Like you did?"

"Of course I did. And I'm serious that you owe me a heist."

I shook my head and stared at the ground for a few seconds before looking up again. "Will I ever talk you out of it?"

Lily grinned. "Never."

"Fine," I said. "But first, I have a different job to do. And for that, I'll need four keys. Do you think you can help me with that?"

Her eyes lit up a bit. "Okay. Keys to what?"

"I need access to four different abandoned buildings and to one place that isn't fully emptied out, but isn't bustling with people, either."

"So, five keys then?" She'd pulled a tiny composition book from her purse and made notes in a cryptic script.

I took a moment to think through my options. "Yes. And burn that page when you no longer need it."

She nodded. "Of course. But why so many?"

I paused. "Do you trust me?"

She stared at me for a long time.

I grinned. "And rightfully you shouldn't. But do you trust me to plan out this little intrigue of ours in such a way that protects us both from being connected to it in the end?"

She nodded quickly. "For that, I trust you."

"Then don't ask questions. The less you know and the less I say, the better."

She paused. "How will I know when it's done?"

"He'll be gone. You'll know because no one in the world will ever see him again."

Lily smiled, though her next words were heavy with bitterness. "And the world will be a better place for it."

"Glad to be of service," I said, just dryly enough to make her bitter smile widen.

I hadn't planned on walking back by my house that night, but the path from the park to the house was so ingrained that I found myself on Baker Street and almost to my front steps right as the sun was starting to set. I might have run right up to the front door if I hadn't heard my father's voice filter through the curtains at the open kitchen window.

"Mori did all that? My Mori?"

I glanced up and down the street as subtly as I could and then pulled down my cap to cover my eyes. I was tempted to pull my hood up as well, but I'd heard the ladies of the neighborhood spouting off enough about the "delinquents in the park with their caps and hoods" to know that might draw more attention to me than I wanted.

So I pulled out my phone and leaned back against my house as close to the window as I dared, then started to twirl a lock of hair around my finger as I pretended to text with one thumb.

"I would have loved to see that bitch's face when she realized."

The longish silence that followed his words made my heart sink a little. I was hoping to find out who he was talking to about me, but he was apparently on the phone.

"And she's done in? You saw the light go out?"

"Yeah, you'll get your extra money. I just need to know for sure she's not recoverin' somewhere. Can't have anyone fighting me for my boys. Fake aunt or no."

Alice. He was talking about Alice, which meant that she was dead. That bang. The smear on Trent's jacket. My dad had arranged for her to die, and whoever he'd hired had used the confusion I created to take his shot. He'd had someone there at the farm after all. Though that didn't make sense to me, because he could have sent someone for the boys at any time.

Only he couldn't without causing a custody mess, which might interfere with his court bail—especially if Alice were to accuse him of kidnapping right before his trial.

He slammed his fist down on the kitchen table, and I heard what sounded like a bottle clank onto its side. My father was practically in tears when he said, "It ain't right that a father has to fight for custody of his own blood."

He was drunk, which made me relax a little. Even if he saw me outside this window right now, he'd probably never believe it was me in the morning. Still, I kept watch for a nosy neighbor or two, while secretly hoping whoever was on the other end of the line would break the news to him about my brothers being lost to him forever in America. I could even talk myself into peering into the window to see his reaction to that.

I thought I might even get my wish with his next question. "And you know where they are, my boys?"

But when I did peek in, he wasn't angry or sad. The lids

on his sunken eyes were drooping and he had this goofy wide grin. He was satisfied with the answer he got.

"Impossible," I whispered, then leaned back to make sure he couldn't see me.

"I'll send the rest of your money tonight, and you'll get a bonus if you can find out the name of the school and get me that address."

He hung up soon after that, but I was stuck there in front of my house, my brain a jumble of all the things I could and should do with this new information. I could stake him out, my dad. Follow him to whomever he was paying off—unless he was just transferring the money online. I could sneak into his house, check his computer history, which would mean luring him away and guessing at his passwords. It was no use. I could follow my father for the next month and never know who he was working with—not if they kept things to phone calls and wire transfers.

And in the meantime, whoever this bastard was who had killed Alice and probably Grady as well, I realized. . . . Yes. That explained why Alice had been so upset. She knew my father was coming for her. And the guy who did her in? He was looking for my brothers.

Something he wouldn't care anything about if my dad were dead. If he knew he'd not get his money for the task, I'd bet he'd give it up in a second.

That meant my time as a watcher was up.

I glanced back into what little I could see of the kitchen as I walked away and then actually typed in a text.

I need those keys tomorrow. No later.

Lily responded in about thirty seconds.

Done.

Lily came through. The next morning, after breakfast, I found a little bag of keys at the base of her father's tree. I sent Lily a picture of the bag, and she reciprocated with a list of addresses.

The first two places I scouted were useless—one was on the verge of becoming rubble and the other was filled with so much rubbish, a person could barely walk through. But the third of the keys Lily gave me was for a boarded-up nursery school with an overgrown play yard out front. It was in Harrow, which was a bit of a distance from our neighborhood but not too far from London proper. It would be an easier lure than some of the other addresses on my list, for sure.

After wrestling with the tiny wooden gate for a few minutes, it finally came free from enough of the vines that had grown through the boards to let me into the yard itself. I tromped through knee-high vegetation to reach a cement patio covered by an open awning. The awning had probably once provided shade under a cheery, multicolored cloth, but now it was nothing but metal bars and fragments of canvas that were bleached white by the sun.

I liked the place instantly. There was something incredibly nonthreatening about it, despite the graffiti warnings and the way even a light wind made the playground equipment squeak and moan. Not only that, but there was an easy path in from the street and into the building itself. The boards on the windows still held strong, which meant anything that happened inside was hidden from the road completely.

The interior of the building was filled with more graffiti and various paraphernalia to indicate a few people may have been using the place as a squat. I kicked an empty bottle of butane across the floor and it rolled into a pile of broken green glass that looked like it had once been a liquor bottle of some kind.

It was the perfect building for an assassination. Easily destroyed, the fire easily blamed on a nameless homeless squatter, and it was outside the Westminster borough, which meant none of my father's lackeys would be called to the scene.

I'd found my killing floor.

I was prepared to see Sherlock again. I really believed that.

And I managed to hold this belief as Lock left his house and stepped down onto the busy sidewalk. He started to walk toward my house, but stopped short and spun around in place to head the other way. That was when I noticed he was being followed. A man wearing a beanie and sunglasses stopped walking the exact moment Lock did, and pretended to be reading something on his phone as Lock moved past him. But the man didn't let Lock get more than five or six steps away before he turned to weave through the crowd as well, following three or four lengths behind Lock.

I could only think of two people who might be interested in tracking Sherlock on a school day, but while Mycroft had the manpower to have his brother's movements monitored, I didn't suppose his men would be as sloppy as the bloke practically tripping over himself to keep up with Lock's tall strides. Only my father would have such an incompetent on the task. And if I hadn't guessed he was one of my father's men before, as they came up parallel to where I was standing across the street, I could tell he was wearing his police uniform pants.

I shook my head. "Bad form."

So, my dad knew I was in town. Or at least he expected I would come back to London and thought he could find me by watching Sherlock. That showed some forethought the old drunk hadn't seemed capable of the night before. For just a moment I thought about walking away from Lock that day. If I never approached him, I could keep my father in the dark for as long as I wanted. I could follow the man trailing Lock and maybe learn what I needed to force my father's hand.

But I didn't have the time for that, and there was an easier way. I slid my hand into my pocket to check on the card I'd drawn up the night before with the address to the nursery school. I'd been looking for a way to make sure my father found it—a way that piqued his interest without making him too suspicious. And seeing Lock's stalker gave me an idea. A plan formed in my head within seconds as I stood there. It was simple and clean and would give me complete control over the time and place of my father's death. The only drawback was I'd have to use Lock to do it.

I warred with that thought as Lock crossed the street to just a few feet from where I stood, his dutiful follower crossing behind. Neither of them saw me at first, though I wasn't really hiding—more standing out of the way. And they both might have passed me by completely, but seeing Lock that close made it impossible for me to stay still.

"Do you not even recognize me on the street? Has it been so long as that?"

Lock stopped midstep, but said nothing. I waited, though, because the twitch of his brow and movement of his lips made me think he had something to say.

When he still didn't speak, I said, "You looked for me."

"You were in my room."

"I was."

We stood in silence, me in shadow and him staring forward, connected only by all the questions he wasn't asking, like where had I been? Why hadn't I met him that day? Why was I back? Was I going to stay in London?

He asked none of that, and still my mouth was filled with the answers. I wanted to tell him. It was all I wanted to say. But then Lock suddenly faced me, and my mind fell blank. I'd prepared myself to see him, but I wasn't at all prepared for him to see me. And for the briefest of moments his eyes held a rush of emotions—far too many for me to decipher. Then they were gone, his expression neutral. He studied me, and though I tried to pretend he was making sure I was still all in one piece, I was forced to remind myself that he had no reason to think otherwise. He had no way of knowing where I'd been, or why. And I no longer had the words to explain it to him.

"You don't look different," he said at last. "Why wouldn't I recognize you?"

He was being purposely cold. So different from how he'd spoken to my name on his map. I felt my own expression soften as I took a step toward him. My father's man had relocated up the street a bit where he could have clearly seen me, even standing out of the way, but I didn't want him to think I was hiding, either.

"Ah, you've noticed my tail," Lock said. "I assume he's been following me around for this exact occasion."

"Maybe."

"And that's why you're here, then? To get your father's attention?"

I paused too long before I said, "I have many reasons to be here."

"And your reasons . . ." Lock trailed off, frowning.

I stepped closer, desperate to know what he was going to say. Was he going to ask my reasons? Should I just give him the answers? Would it matter?

He turned to face the street. "Well, you've accomplished at least one of your goals. Glad I could help."

I thought he might simply stride off, disappear into the crowd, but I wasn't ready for him to go. Was that why I was involving Lock in all of this? To keep him near me just a few more hours? Would I really weave him into the web I'd use to catch a monster just for that? Was I truly that selfish?

"My other reasons," I blurted. "I'd like to tell you." I willed him to answer. When he did not, I added, "I'd like to tell you everything."

He kept his eyes trained forward, but he nodded once to let me know he would listen.

"There's a derelict nursery school in Harrow. I'll be there tomorrow morning." I rummaged in my pocket for the card with the address, then held it up between us. Lock carefully read the paper without ever making eye contact with me, then turned away. I tried to push the address back into my pocket, purposely missing. The card fell perfectly to the ground, just behind Lock so that he couldn't see, and beneath my arm so that I wouldn't be expected to see either. Though I did note the slight grin on the face of my father's man.

Lock caught me spying on his stalker and cleared his throat to bring my attention back to him.

"Will you be there?" I asked.

"With or without my tail?"

We both gave in to smiles, and he tilted his head just enough to meet my eyes.

I said, "I trust you'll manage to ditch that old man."

"Sounds like a bit of fun. I'm in."

I held his gaze for a few seconds more than I should have, which was undoubtedly why it hurt so much to look away.

Chapter 13

Some days require bloodred lipstick. Perhaps it would have been smarter if I'd tried to make sure I wore nothing that would stand out. No jewelry, no name brands, only bland colors, and makeup designed to help obscure my facial features. But I wasn't so interested in taking the smarter path on that day. I wore lavish makeup and a bright white sundress that I'd seen in a shop window near my hotel. It looked just like one my mum had worn when I was small. I even pulled out my mum's rubies from the tiny metal trinkets box I'd found among her things. I'd spent months thinking through what was about to happen, and I was going to enjoy it fully, with no restrictions or hesitation.

I clasped the ruby pendant at my neck, put on the matching dangle earrings, and tucked my hair behind one ear to show them off. I wanted my father to see them. To see me in her clothes, wearing her things. Because if my mum had been half the woman I was, she would have taken care of this chore long ago.

But when I wandered past the mirror, I caught myself

scowling, which really wouldn't do. I corrected my expression immediately as I pulled on white lace gloves. No anger or irritation allowed. I forced a smile that made my lower lip shine red and full in the mirror. That was exactly how I wanted to see myself when I faced him—how I wanted him to see me.

Gloriously happy.

My happiness would be the last thing he ever saw.

My smile was more natural as I entered the nursery school for the second time that morning. I set down my bag and overcoat on an old dusty counter by the front door and looked around. It was perfect. All the work was done. Today would change everything.

I felt light. Almost cheery. And seeing that Sherlock was already there, standing in the very center of the main room, made my smile widen. "I wasn't sure I'd actually see you today."

"I said I'd be here." His eyes lit up as he took in my outfit, but there was a hint of confusion in his expression as well. "It appears I'm underdressed." He straightened the tie of his school uniform.

"Your clothes don't matter." I started to say something else, but a familiar voice called out from the back room.

"Do mine?"

I managed to keep my smile, despite my father's confident strides into the room. He looked older than he should—as if the five months of my absence had accelerated his aging. His eyes were more sunken, or perhaps the skin around them was darker. His hair was lighter with gray. He was even dressed like an old man: his trousers just a bit too baggy and pooling at his ankles, a wrinkled dress shirt peeking out from a cardigan sweater that was so tight, the buttons stretched their holes at his gut, which was much more pronounced than I'd noticed through the window. But his steps were light as he positioned himself between Lock and me, then started to laugh.

"Hello, Moriarty," he said. I was surprised at how little his presence affected the dank room where we stood. He was just another scurrying pest, really. Something to be stomped out or scared away. I knew I was ready to face him when the heat in my core stripped away all the lightness I'd felt in seeing Lock, until I was this dark, angry thing—exactly what I needed to be to face him. I was running on rage. This was the man who'd held my mum captive, who'd beaten my brothers bloody. This was the man who had terrified Michael so much that he ran out into the street to his ruin, who'd strangled me and taken away my only friend. And this man was about to pay for what he'd done.

"Where are the others?" I asked.

"Others? Who else would come to a dump like this but me?"

I stepped toward my father as I spoke. "Those pathetic little rats who scurry after you wherever you go and flash their bloodstained badges as they run your errands."

He started a smile that turned to a sneer when he backhanded me. Sherlock lurched forward, but I held up a hand to stop him and smiled at both of them as I thumbed blood from the corner of my mouth and watched it seep into the white lace of my glove.

"That was just starting to heal—"

My father spoke over me. "You watch how you speak to me, girl!"

"Do you expect me to believe you'd come here by yourself?"

He narrowed his eyes and started to respond. "I don't need help dealing with a filthy cow like—"

Sherlock interrupted. "You didn't ask how he found you." He paused like he was waiting for an answer, but not long enough to actually hear one from me. "You didn't ask how he got here. Because you knew. You told him how to find us?"

My father seemed overly pleased by this development and pulled a piece of paper from his pocket. He tossed it to the ground, but it flipped before it hit so that instead of the address, the paper only showed the rather ornate *M* I'd drawn on the back. The liquid in a nearby puddle started to absorb into the paper, drawing out the ink. "Tried to make it look like an accident, she did. But I wasn't fooled."

"You weren't meant to be fooled," I said.

"But I was?" Lock had all my father's attention then, but I couldn't look at him. I had other things to think about, and he was playing his part well enough. I sidestepped to keep my father between us.

"He's seeing it all, Mori, just the kind of person you are. And now that he knows . . . well, what did I tell you?"

"That he could never love me," I said, feeding him the line to keep him talking. If I could just keep his eyes trained on Sherlock, this would all be over quickly.

He turned his gaze to me. "That no one ever will," he corrected. He paused just long enough to take in the fake sadness in my expression, then swung back to watch Lock. It was all a part of his mental games, I knew. He had to prove to me that he wasn't the least bit afraid of me. That I didn't matter enough to even warrant his attention. He had to show me I was nothing.

And that provided the perfect opportunity.

I reached just under the hem of my dress to unsnap the holds on the sheath tied around my thigh. I felt the weight of the dagger in my hand and heard it slide free.

But he didn't. He was too busy blathering on about how Lock should stay far away from me if he were smart. I approached my father from behind, my knife ready, my mind clear. And then, when I was close enough to see over his shoulder, I saw the sword in his hand, pointed directly at Lock's chest.

I must have made some kind of startled noise, because he said, "That's right. Put your weapon down, girl. You didn't think I'd come here without some protection for myself." When I didn't obey him immediately, he added, "Unless you think you are faster than me," and with a flick of his wrist the sword tip was at Lock's throat.

In the space of a breath, I let the contingencies of the situation play out in my mind. I had only two options. I could drop my dagger, and my father would either kill Sherlock directly just to spite me, or use his sword to corral me to Lock's side, where he would try to kill us both or run. Either way, I'd be weaponless and at his mercy. I could refuse, and he could kill Sherlock, but before he recovered, my dagger would be in his heart. Or I might beat him. If I were fast enough and pulled him back against me, I might be able to kill him before he could do anything to Lock.

Either way Lock might die, or he might not, but my father wouldn't die if I dropped the knife. So obviously I had to keep it.

"No," I said, and I pressed the point of my dagger into the small of his back before he could move an inch.

"I said I'll kill him." My father's stance projected confidence, but his voice was strained, his laughter forced. "She doesn't seem to care much for you, boy."

Lock's expression was calm, but his eyes were bright in that way they always were when he was learning something new.

"You'll kill him?" I asked my father. "Then what?"

"Then he'll be dead, you cow. Is that what you want?"

"That would change things. Probably not in a way you'd like." I shifted my own stance so I could place a hand on my father's shoulder. "I was going to kill you quickly, but you're forcing me to make certain adjustments." Was it the gentle tone of my voice that made Lock's fascination give way to fear? His eyes had lost their light.

"Detective Moriarty," I said, "let me explain to you what happens next. The moment I see a drop of that boy's blood, this knife goes into your spine. At this angle, I'll probably injure you at T7, maybe T8."

My father took a shallow breath but said nothing. Lock was studying me in that way that made me think he could see into my mind, so I grinned at him and winked, sending his scrutiny into overdrive. Perhaps the blood dripping down my chin ruined the effect.

"Do you know what that kind of injury will do to you?" I asked quietly into my father's ear.

He flinched, which only widened my smile. I could taste blood on my teeth.

"You'll lose control of your bowels and bladder, lose control of your legs." I slid my hand down to reach under his arm and around his chest to pull him tight to my body, then dug the tip of my knife into his back.

His arm moved up in sync with my movements, pushing his sword tip into Sherlock's skin. "Let me go, or I'll kill him."

I raised a brow at Lock. "What do you think?"

Lock's gaze pierced into my eyes, making it near impossible to hold my amusement. But I did my best, even when he said, "Don't do this."

My father started to chuckle roughly, most likely thinking Lock was pleading with him, but I knew better. I also knew no amount of pleading would change the results of what happened next. I hoped the two of us would eventually walk out of the school, but my father never would. That I was sure of.

My expression must have given me away, because Sherlock's became much more frantic. "Mori."

"Then kill him," I said to my father, though I pulled him

back to release the tension of the blade at Lock's neck. "Kill him, and instead of killing you in return, maybe I leave you here with a severed spine. Lock you in this building for a few days with only the rats and the puddles to sustain you, dragging your useless legs around and shouting for help. And if no one can hear you?" I quieted my voice further. "If you're still here when I get back, I promise you, I'll have devised a most painful way for you to die."

I heard the clang of his sword falling to the ground, and watched his hands slide into the air. I couldn't help myself; I started to laugh. And the sound of it brought relief to Lock's face, and even made my father join in, though his laughter was nervous and short-lived.

"I dropped my weapon," he practically whined. But I didn't remove my knife from his back.

"You are such a coward," I said. "Though we knew that, didn't we?"

My father started going on again, with his self-indulgent whining. Perhaps he was even attempting to be clever and find a way out. I didn't really hear all that he was saying, but I did hear his last word. As I pulled the weapon from his back to sweep across his neck, I heard him say one final word, and then nothing ever again.

"Mori—"

He said my name. There was something delicious about that. And kind of hilarious, really. So as his blood sprayed out to pepper Lock's shirt and tie in red, as his disgusting dirty body fell to its knees and then forward right into a puddle on the cement, I kept laughing. It was a breathy, stuttered laugh, full of shock and bewilderment, but still a laugh.

"Mori," I whispered, cutting the *i* sound short, then laughed a little more. "I couldn't have planned for that."

I reached down to clean my blade using the back of my father's shirt, but then decided not to waste too much time on it. The dagger would be melted to molten metal soon enough. I was trying to decide whether to re-sheath it or not when a blood-speckled hand grabbed my wrist just above the lace glove that was now almost completely red.

"Why?" Lock asked. And the look he gave me shook me free from all my posturing. I couldn't even hold my smile. Not anymore. How could he undo me like that? With nothing but a mere look?

"Don't," I said, pleading. Because I'd been prepared for his anger at my betrayal. I was ready for him to hate me, for his features to twist in wretched disgust once he saw me for who I really was. But I couldn't move for what I saw in his eyes just then.

He glanced up from our hands and forced me to see it again—his fear. Not blank like all those times he feared for himself. Not fear of the moment, like the expression he wore when we were about to embark on an adventure. He was afraid *for* me—concern, pain, grief, and loss. I tried to break free of him, but he clung to me like he was afraid I'd run away. And then his hands came up to circle my face and he asked, "Where were you all those months you were gone?"

I breathed out a laugh. "You're asking me now? I was ready

to tell you all about it yesterday. Where were your questions then?"

Sherlock looked at his hands and released me suddenly. He tried to brush the blood away but only managed to smear it. "What has happened to you?"

"This has always been me, Sherlock." I watched him shake his head, his eyes jetting around like he was looking for some proof that I was lying. Was I lying? "Did you really think you could tell everything about me from those silly deductions of yours?"

"You killed him like it was nothing."

"It *was* nothing. He was nothing." I sidestepped until he was forced to meet my eyes again. "Did you really think I could leave? Did you not know I'd come back for this?" I gestured at the body on the floor. "This right here was always my destiny."

"I—I don't believe in destiny."

I might have smiled if I weren't so lost in the emptiness I felt. "Neither do I. But I suppose that doesn't really matter now." I did smile then—felt the flicker of something pulling at me, luring me away from that place and the man who could no longer hurt us. "I don't suppose anything really does."

I took a step back and watched Lock's reaction. He was still confused, like his mind was trying to rationalize how he could have been so wrong about something. I'd done that. I'd broken him in so many ways. I took another couple of steps back and then stopped in front of one of the larger puddles on the ground. There was a slightly sweet smell to it—to the whole place really. It was a wonder Lock hadn't noticed on his way inside.

I glanced up just in time to watch his transformation from bumbling shock to devastation.

He took a step toward me. "I have to bring you in, tell the police what you've done." I wasn't sure which broke him more, those words or everything that had come before. But he was a pane of shattered glass that even the slightest breeze might scatter to the floor. And I was the big bad wolf come to blow down his house.

I briefly wondered if he'd ever truly know how deeply all those shards would cut me—how I already felt all of them.

"I have to call the police," he said.

"You won't."

"I have to. I have to stop you."

I forced my smile back into place despite the shimmering pain inside me. "Okay, then. Stop me. But you'll have to prove I'm guilty first."

I flicked open a lighter with the hand still gloved in white and tossed it on the pile of rubble I'd arranged. I stayed only long enough to add my gloves to the pile and watch the fire catch, and to see Sherlock realize that the puddles that had separated us in this room weren't made of water. Then I left.

He might have died in that old nursery school. Or not. I couldn't be sure, but then, I didn't figure that was how the brilliant Sherlock Holmes would die. Today was about the death of a monster . . . and perhaps the birth of another. I was the phoenix, climbing from the ashes of my father. Only I was a new creature altogether. And as much as Sherlock tried, he would never be able to stop me.

Chapter 14

It wasn't enough. I'd thought killing the man at the center of all our problems would be the end of it. I'd planned for everything—avoiding the CCTV as I left Harrow, dropping the knife I'd used into a vat of molten metal at a local artisan's forge, burning my bloody clothes and shoes in an old basement furnace at a hotel in Chelsea. My crime was clean. Untraceable. I'd thought I could make my way into obscurity, sell off my house, and then leave for the States. But it seemed my father had found a way to torture me, even from the grave.

The first *M* came with the post.

I wasn't even meant to be there, in *my* house—the one my father had polluted with his belongings and bottles in the months I was gone. Not that I'd seen any of that right away. Later, I would find piles of empty bottles in my brothers' rooms. I'd find that he'd brought all the stuff in the attic down to make his room look like a hoarder's paradise, full of memories of his life with my mum. Later, I'd see the way he'd shredded my mattress and the clothes I'd left behind with the shards of broken bottles. He'd used my brothers' rooms to mourn and mine to live out his violent fantasies. Our house had become the living metaphor of his breakdown.

But I saw none of it at first, and that was his fault as well. Because it smelled like him the moment I walked in the door—not cologne, just alcohol and sweat and his deodorant and him. He'd smelled of it when I'd pulled him close to slash his neck, and then he'd smelled only of blood.

Blood that speckled Lock's hands for standing too close.

Blood that Lock couldn't wipe away.

The clank of the post-slot door jolted me from my memory, and I might have just ignored the bills and advertisements falling on top of the pile of untouched mail my father had left behind, but then the slot clanked again, this time dropping only one piece of mail. A postcard, with a large, ornate *M* drawn across the front. It wasn't the exact art that I'd used on my father's invitation to his demise, but it was a clear, though rather sloppy, imitation. I stared at it for a few seconds too long, so that by the time I lifted the card from the floor, it was too late to run out the door and see who had left it for me.

I saw what you did. You can buy my silence.

The message on the back didn't surprise me much, though the address he'd scrawled underneath it did. My blackmailer wanted me to return to the scene of the crime. And he wanted me there that night.

It was a slightly clever plan. The site would be near swarming with London civil service. The fire brigade would have called in police as soon as they found what remained of my father's body. If my blackmailer were part of the police force, as I could only suspect he was, my returning to the scene would make me a prime suspect, even if I paid him off, which would put me under his thumb for the rest of our lives. If I refused to show, I was sure he would manufacture some kind of evidence that would prove the ashes and bones belonged to my father and then the fingers would all point at me. Either way I had to be in Harrow that night, but somehow Mori couldn't be there.

That was easy enough.

I texted Lily. *I need you to let me into the school theater. Side door, where no one can see.*

And then I grabbed my bag and left.

I managed to get to the school just before the last bell rang for lunch, which left me almost an hour to get what I needed.

Lily was at the door as promised. "What happened? Did it go wrong?"

The scent of my father came back to me there at the theater side door, as did the memory of him falling forward, of Sherlock's speckled hands. I shook my head and blinked it away. "No." I met Lily's gaze. "It's done."

I watched the relief break through her longing and wondered briefly when I'd get to feel that for myself.

Lily looked around her and pulled me inside, and then she snuck me down to the basement stairs. I nodded in thanks, but she put out a hand to stop me from going. So we stood there in this awkward space for a few seconds, and just when I started to say that I was in a rush, she interrupted me.

"I'm starting it up again, Sorte Juntos. Just as Alice planned, only here in London." She waited for my reaction, and when I didn't give one, she added, "You should join me."

"I can't. I'll be in America soon."

"You should put that off a few months and join me. For your mother."

I felt my body shift toward her at the mention of my mum, and my expression must have given away my sudden rise of anger, because Lily's hand instinctively grabbed for the banister.

"Going to America is what I am doing for my mum. And I'm doing it with the money she earned running that little club of thieves."

"I'm sorry. I didn't mean—"

"Don't do it."

Lily's gaze snapped up to meet mine. "I'm doing this for my own reasons. And I can do it with or without you."

"What do you need? Money? I'll give you money. Is it because you believed Alice after all? Don't. She was a deluded con artist. None of her plans would ever have worked. She never had my mum's skills, no matter how much she wished otherwise."

"It's not about Alice or the money. It's my legacy."

I shook my head. "You don't have the people to pull it off, and you can't trust anyone connected to her. Promise me you won't."

Lily looked away from me and started fiddling with the strap on her handbag. "You have somewhere to be?"

I gave her a few more seconds of my attention and then disappeared down the stairs. I couldn't take on her troubles.

I had plenty of my own, and only a short time to pilfer the things that I needed.

Pretty much every part of the theater basement that wasn't Lock's lab was storage for the school's ancient relics. A good half of those were boxes of costumes and other sundry accessories from past theater productions. It took nearly the entire hour to sift through the mothball-scented polyester and chiffon. Still, I managed to find a couple of wigs and a long black coat that would disguise the shape of my body as well as most of my clothing. That, together with the newer box of stage makeup I found near the door, gave me all the tools I'd need to get ready for that night.

I paused briefly in the basement hallway to stare at the closed doors of Lock's lab. And for just that one moment, I felt a tug somewhere inside of me to step closer. Even when I turned my back, even when I walked resolutely for the stairs, I felt so drawn to the far end of the hall, I couldn't seem to force myself up one step. And when I turned back, I was flooded with memory—of Lock's eyes, bright with discovery as his experiment surprised him. The rosy pink of his cheeks when he caught me staring. The sound of his chair wheeling toward me across the carpet. The scent of him surrounding me as his thumb traced my cheek and his lips touched to mine.

I found a smile on my own lips, but when I closed my eyes against the ache of that, I could only see the brokenness of Lock's expression standing in a derelict nursery school, the blood spatter on his hands. Even now, I could picture him sitting in the dark among all his experiments and equipment and books, but I couldn't guess what he'd be thinking. Was he forming a plan to catch me and turn me in to the police for what I'd done? Was he afraid of me? Was he trying to figure out why I'd made him a witness to my crime?

Did I know why myself?

I walked up the first five steps to escape that question, and then ran the rest of the way until I was out the side door and away from that basement for good. I didn't have time for nostalgia or regrets. I had to focus on right now—on whoever was trying to blackmail me and how I could end this mess to reunite with my brothers. That was all I could afford to think about. Everything else was for later.

I was perhaps being too cautious, but every time I mentally ran through my plan to find out who had sent me that note, my mind would spin out a dozen contingencies, which made me exceedingly uncomfortable. But it would work. It had to work. And I needed only one more piece to bring it all together.

So I sent another text, this time to the most brilliant hacker I knew.

I returned to the hotel with two hours to spare and a smile on my face. Jason Kim was as charming as ever, and his growing romance with Kay, the girl who'd almost gotten him kicked out of school over a mobile phone, made him an exceptionally worthwhile resource.

"It's on me," he'd said when I'd tried to offer him money for his services.

"Let me at least pay you for the phones."

"Nope. I couldn't pay you back if I tried. The very least I can do is give you a couple of old phones."

"Equipped with your clever tracker."

He grinned. "So, who's the target this time? Another nefarious police matter?"

"That's top secret, I'm afraid. And it's nothing so exciting as last time. I promise."

Jason paused. "And you're doing it all on your own?"

I did my best to keep my expression neutral. "Yes, well, some things are best handled alone, don't you think?"

He considered that, but it evidently didn't change his mind. "He missed you."

"I doubt that." I looked out the window. I didn't doubt. I knew. But Sherlock wouldn't want anything to do with me ever again. My father would prove to be right after all.

"I was helping him, you know. To find you while you were gone."

"I know he searched. But things have changed. Neither of us are the people we were before."

Jason crossed his arms and shook his bangs out of his eyes. "He still is. He called me just last night to see if I could locate your new phone."

"Don't tell him," I blurted.

Jason's brows came together.

"I can't let him be a part of this. I'm protecting him. You understand that."

He nodded, though I was sure he'd relent to Lock's requests

eventually. Jason Kim was the prince of romantic gestures, after all. And being in love makes people think everyone else should be as well. It also turns most people into idiots.

"This is how you can repay me," I said before I left. "By not telling Lock that you've seen me. Promise me that and we'll be even."

"We'll never be even," he said with a smile that showed off his perfect teeth. "But you have my word."

I wanted to believe he'd keep it. At least for the night. The very last thing I needed was for Sherlock to show up and ruin everything. *Or maybe he wouldn't recognize me either*, I thought, as I gathered my costume pieces and supplies on my hotel bed.

I started with the ginger wig. It was cheap, which meant it had all the realism of a clown wig, despite the relatively natural color of the hair. I took an hour or so to update the cut, using an old brown mascara to darken the roots at the part and some dry shampoo to dull the plastic shine of the hair. I put my own hair up in a loose bun that would allow me to tuck it under the wig, and could be easily taken down once I removed it.

Next was clothing. Nothing recognizable, no logos or brand names. I wore a black T-shirt and my plainest jeans, then white trainers—the kind that could be purchased almost anywhere. No jewelry that might fall off, no perfume that someone might remember later, and then the large trench coat. I wore dark brown gloves, heavy makeup, and fake glasses with thick enough frames to help obscure the actual shape of my eyes.

I didn't put the wig or glasses on until I was off my bus in Harrow. I waited until I was mostly alone on the street, then ducked down a side alley to finish my disguise. I turned on the tiny burner phone Jason had provided and pocketed it to make it easily accessible. And when everything was as ready as it could be, I made my way back to the one place I thought I'd never show my face again.

I saw the glow of the work lights illuminating the site before I crested the hill. I'd been right about the number of civil servants surrounding the place. What I hadn't counted on was the level of chaos at the scene. Unlike all the crime scenes I'd seen in London, this one wasn't taped off nicely, nor was there a decent perimeter of officers to stop the public from wandering too close. I was trying to decide if this would work in my favor or not when I spotted my blackmailer.

He made it too easy, really. We were a good forty-five minutes and at least three boroughs from West End Central Police Station, which meant I shouldn't have recognized any of the police on the scene. But the officer who was trying to push the crowd back from between two fire trucks wore an unmistakable sneer—Officer Parsons, the man who had stalked and terrorized Michael and caused his accident.

My body shifted very naturally into my fighter's stance, and I felt my hands ball into fists just at the sight of him. It took almost a full minute of focus to keep from launching straight at him to make him pay.

But I had to wait. I had to be smart about it. Take my time.

And when it was time? I would see him beg for mercy.

I stepped forward to test myself, stopping when I felt my jaw clench. Then I moved closer still, to acclimate to the sound of his pathetic voice. I had to control everything about myself, from my shaking fists balled at my side to the twitch in my lip that was threatening to curl and reveal my rage. I had to be neutral to approach him, and I had to do it quickly and get out of there.

When Parsons was done lecturing a kid Freddie's age about how he should be home in bed, I moved in. I slid my burner phone into the pocket of his coat while he looked at the site. When he turned back toward me, I held a card between us, my properly drawn *M* on the side facing him. Which meant the message side was facing me.

The payment you requested is waiting for you on your front porch.

He snatched the card from me, and I took the time he spent reading the back to escape into the crowd. I managed to find a place to hide just in time to watch him step out from behind a sloppily hung piece of crime scene tape to search for me. And when he couldn't find me, he checked his watch and then grinned. As I walked to the street to catch a black cab, I checked my phone to make sure his little blue dot moved slowly away from the nursery school. He was heading home, and I would see him there.

Chapter 15

Officer Parsons lived in a terraced house in Hertfordshire. I thought I was angry when I saw his sneering face at the burnt-out nursery school, but something about his tall, expertly manicured hedge and the row of lovely flowering bulbs near his front door made me clench my jaw as I crossed the street. I didn't see him until I was almost to his front walk. He was waiting for me, looking like he'd already won. It was the expression my father wore when I'd gone to visit him in jail, the same he'd had when he sauntered into the nursery school to take his punishment.

And it stopped me on the threshold of Parsons's front garden.

"Who's this, then?" he asked.

I pulled off my wig and glasses and slid the trench coat from my shoulders.

"You?" The word was formed as a question, but felt more like an accusation. "I don't remember requesting you."

I dropped the wig and trench coat just inside the hedge, and then I paused. It wasn't that I couldn't move forward, it was that

I knew when I did, I wouldn't be able to stop myself again, and something about the recklessness I felt made me wait.

"All right, then. Where's this payment of mine? Give it over."

His lips stretched in a wide, confident grin, and I wondered, was that how he'd smiled at Michael when he'd followed the boys home from school? I could see it in my head, Parsons donning this expression just as he stopped the van to grab Freddie and Seanie off the street. In my vision, he watched Michael run off into traffic. He could have stopped it. He could have stopped all of it.

That scenario and a dozen more like it tainted my thoughts like ink in water until they were all dark and dim. He didn't seem so imposing in this residential paradise, in his uniform, with that grin. But here was the monster who had driven my brother to flee in panic. He was the one who'd stolen away the brother I knew and left a vacant, smiling boy in his place. He was the cause of Michael's pain, his seizures and shakes, his night terrors.

He'd hurt Michael.

"It's right here," I said through clenched teeth, and then I took a step forward.

The pure hatred I felt must have shown on my face, because Parsons reached behind to open his front door like he would escape inside. My amusement at his fear didn't seem to quell his worries.

"What's right here? You stay there and tell me."

I paused. "Me. I'm your payment."

I didn't hear what he said next. My rage roared like a storm in my ears, pushing me forward, always forward. I must have moved faster than he expected, because he'd only backed a few steps into his house when I reached him. I used my momentum and swung my clasped hands right for his temple. I thought for sure he would block the hit, but he looked confused when it connected, like he hadn't seen it coming. He stumbled a few steps to the right, then reached a hand out to steady himself against a wall. I ran up to strike again, but he recovered more quickly than I'd guessed and shot an arm out to punch me in the stomach.

I was winded but still managed another blow to his face, which knocked him into the edge of a shelving unit in the hall. Whether from my fist or the wood, he got a small gash above his eye, but that didn't stop him from fighting back, and soon he managed to pin me to the wall, his hand at my throat.

He wasn't confused anymore. Though when he brought his face close to mine, I could see he was having a hard time focusing his eyes. "You're in trouble now, girly. You shouldn't have come here."

I scratched at his hand, but he held firm and slammed me back against the wall again. I kneed him in the groin and he tossed me to the ground. I spun away as quickly as I could to avoid any possible kicks or stomps, but he wasn't coming for me. He staggered to the side, giving me just enough time to recover into a crouch. I couldn't let the opportunity pass, so I jumped up and slammed my fists down on his shoulders as hard as I could, pushing him to his knees. I jumped on his back, wrapping my arm around his neck, and held as tight as I could. He tried to yell, but the sound came out strangled. He tried to pull at my arms, but I didn't give an inch. He even tried to reach back for my face, but I didn't let go; I leaned back, choking him harder and escaping his clutching fingers, until we both fell to the floor.

It took a long time for him to stop moving, much longer than it had taken with Lucas through the bars all those months ago. But even after he went limp in my arms, I didn't let go. He'd hurt Michael, and making him pass out didn't seem like enough punishment for his crime.

Still, I held on.

I held on when the roar quieted, when I could hear my own heavy breathing again, when I could feel my arm ache from the exertion. And when I finally let go, my whole body shook for a few long seconds, like I was quaking with cold, only I was still heated from the fighting. I pushed his dead weight off me with a whimper and turned to look out through his front door at an empty street. No one had seen or heard. Not yet.

I got up and started for the door, but when I reached for the doorknob, I thought about fingerprints. I looked back at Parsons's prone form and tried to relive the fight just as it had happened. I'd really only been in the hall, and I hadn't touched much, but I needed to be sure.

The texture on the wall would probably have kept my prints from showing there, but I grabbed a rag from under his sink to wipe them down, being careful to use the sleeve of my shirt to open and close things. I found one of those dust mops with a cleaning sprayer and wiped down the floor, then I retrieved my phone from his pocket and used the rag again to wipe around his neck and face and the skin of his hands and arms. I even scraped my skin from under his fingernails.

When I was putting everything away, I found his mail scattered on his kitchen table, with a messily drawn *M* postcard right on top.

You'll be paid well for your services, it said on the back.

I knew what it meant almost immediately. He'd gotten a postcard too, which meant he hadn't sent the card to me. I'd been played. And there was one person I knew who'd done this to me before, only that time was with thank-you cards and elaborate drawings of all my sins.

"Alice." I whispered her name into the empty house, but it still didn't make sense. Alice was dead, or at least the person talking to my dad had told him so. And the gunshot? And the blood on Trent's jacket?

If she'd somehow survived and was exacting her revenge, why would she want me to face down Parsons? He wore a uniform. He wasn't some well-placed detective who could make trouble for her down the line. This definitely wasn't her attempt at revenge on me. She had to know I wouldn't have paid off anyone related to my father. And after my training with Trent, I wasn't going to be bested by some bobby.

Regardless of why—if Alice was using me as her tool to get my father's crew out of her way, what could I do about that? And did I want to do anything at all?

Our escape from the farm had been relatively easy, I knew

that, and I'd decided to believe in my own cleverness rather than her treacherous hand. But it was possible she'd set me up, maybe from the beginning, and I'd fallen for it. In my zeal to get my own revenge, I'd let her use me the way she had always intended.

But was she really using me when I was getting what I wanted?

I pocketed the *M* postcard and glanced over my shoulder at the dead body of Officer Parsons. If Alice knew the names and addresses of all of my father's most trusted, maybe I'd let her use me as a sword—for now, anyway.

Chapter 16

My suspicions about Alice were confirmed the next day.

I couldn't sleep much of the night. I kept shaking myself awake out of nightmares about being chased or falling through the floor or not being able to remember something I needed to know to survive. So in the early morning hours I walked back to my house, sat in my mum's room, and went through the boxes my father had brought down from the attic. I didn't know if I was looking for keepsakes or answers or what.

Not that I was particularly nostalgic. But my father had destroyed so much of my mum already. He'd kept her things from us, and I needed to own the rest of it. I wouldn't allow him to succeed in hoarding her all to himself. Plus, it felt wrong, somehow, to leave it all behind without knowing what was inside. Especially because I knew how lovingly my mum had packed it all away. This was what she chose to keep. This was her legacy. And I couldn't leave it to be tossed away by strangers.

I almost changed my mind after the fourth box of baby clothes that I stacked in the rubbish pile. You would have thought my mum had hand sewn these clothes herself for the way she hung on to them. I wasn't sure what part of our childhood was worth remembering so fondly, but I chalked it up to the sentimentality of motherhood and moved on.

I packed photo albums into a nice moving box but stopped short of putting my mum's scrapbook about my father's police achievements on top. I couldn't seem to toss it into the rubbish pile either. It had her handwriting in it. Her work. It was as much a piece of my mum as it was about her husband, though I still couldn't put together why she'd spent time on it at all.

I flipped through page after page, all chronicling what should have been a bright path for a less corrupt copper. She'd even snuck in a couple of articles that seemed to be about criminals who got away, which was odd. Like the Lukin Streeters, a street gang who'd been extorting businesses near Whitechapel to pay protection money. It read like an episode of a bad cop drama, only instead of miraculously finding that one piece of evidence that took them down and locked them up for good, the gang was never seen again, which was bad for justice but good for the people of Whitechapel, who no longer had to fear extortion.

The article had nothing to do with my dad. It wasn't about him receiving an accolade or praise for some good work, but still it was glued beautifully into the book just like all the others, with a date written next to it in my mum's perfectly slanted script. As was the article pasted in three pages later, which was about some kind of drug ring that reportedly used smaller satellite bank locations to launder money. This one had a picture, and I could just make out DS Day standing in full constable uniform in the background. Still, like the other, this story didn't have so much a happy ending as it did just an ending.

No justice, but the bank branches in question were clean as of their last inspections.

After finding two more articles treated in a similar way, I finally settled on a reason why my mum might have immortalized all of it. It was evidence. What would make a gang flee when the law didn't stop its operation? Make a corrupt banker bow to what was right rather than the might of a drug lord?

Perhaps a corrupt band of brothers in blue.

And my mum had chronicled every moment of it, from the mysterious death of the man who had killed Mrs. Greeves's son to the accident that took the life of a well-loved police chief. This scrapbook was a collection of stories about my father, and when I saw them as a list of all my father's crimes and all the ways he had benefited from them, suddenly every page had new meaning. And the worst was what it said about my mum.

All these years, she'd known exactly who my father was.

I caught myself staring at my mum's handwriting because there was something there, something odd. I flipped back to the beginning of the book and then through the pages, only looking at the writing. It was all written with the same pen. And the articles had all aged the same. She hadn't known all along. She'd collected these all at once.

I'd probably never know why, but I could guess. Maybe this was going to be the thing that kept him from following her when she took us and left. Maybe this book was going to be used to force him to leave forever. Regardless, she never used it. And the thought of what could have been made me dump the book on the trash heap. It didn't matter anymore. He was gone and so was she.

I heard the clank of the post slot just as I snatched the book back, and I tossed the thing on my mum's bed to run for the door. But by the time I opened it, whoever had dropped the postcard had also disappeared into the foot traffic on Baker Street. Which left just me and another sloppily drawn *M* in the entry. I thought about tearing it to shreds, packing up my life, and escaping to America to leave it all behind me. But if Alice were alive, she'd find me there. It was her country, after all. And then I'd have put the boys in the middle of it all again.

So I picked up the postcard from the floor and read the first of three phrases on the other side.

I want my money back.

"Alice," I said aloud. She was no longer hiding.

But first you'll do me a favor.

I stared at the writing, trying to remember what Alice's handwriting looked like. But then this was Alice. A grifter, con artist, charlatan. She could write like anybody.

Your next target is murderer Stan Gareth. He killed Grady. He knows where you're hiding your brothers.

"He couldn't," I said aloud. And Alice couldn't be alive. There were too many couldn'ts about this mess, and an address at the bottom of the card, which meant she wanted me to play her assassin once more. Only I barely knew Stan. He wasn't on my list, nor was he part of my father's group of dirty coppers.

He knows where you're hiding your brothers.

I read it again and felt hollow inside. It had been my only solace, that my brothers were safe—out of reach of all this. Far, far away from here. But if someone knew . . .

No. This had to be more of Alice's lies. She was trying to use me again, this time to kill a man who'd worked for—and probably knew too much about—her. This postcard was just another trick. I wouldn't be Alice's pawn. Even if he did know where the boys were, it didn't matter. My father was dead. Alice would eventually out herself. I had other ways of keeping my brothers safe. I wouldn't be bullied into killing anyone I didn't want to. Doing that meant letting her win.

The mail slot clanked again, and I ripped open the door before the postal slot had even shut properly. A young boy, maybe Freddie's age, was staring at me like he was too afraid to stay and too afraid to move at the same time. He started to run down my front steps, but I was faster. I grabbed him by his shirt before he reached the walk and spun him around.

"Who sent you?" I demanded.

He didn't answer, not that I expected him to.

"I'm not going to hurt you. Just tell me who sent you here."

"Dunno. Lady in the park gave me a fiver. Promised me another if I told her how you reacted." Which was why he'd come back. To peek through my mail slot and watch me.

"How was I supposed to react?"

"Said if you didn't look scared, I should give you this."

He held out an envelope. I grabbed it and reached into my

back pocket to pull out all the money I had there. Two ten-pound notes. I offered them to the boy, who tried to snatch them right away, but I held them up. He wasn't so terrified anymore.

"Go get your money and tell her I ripped the letter in two and started to laugh. Tell her I said, 'Pathetic. I'm not her sword.' Got that?"

"Not her sword. Got it."

I handed him the money and he smiled wide enough to show off some gaps in his teeth where they hadn't quite grown back in. Then he ran in the direction of Regent's Park. I thought about following him, but I didn't need to go to Alice. If he passed on my message, she would come to me. Eventually.

I grinned at the thought of Alice's scowl when she heard how little I cared for her lies. I was still grinning when I opened the envelope the boy had delivered, but all of that stopped when I saw what was inside—a Polaroid of Olivia and my brothers all crowded into what looked like first-class seats on a train car. Liv stood in front of the boys, acting as a shield, but she looked scared. So scared. I knew there would be a message on the back, and I knew it would change everything.

Take care of Stan, and I'll drop them off to take their flight at 8 p.m. tomorrow night. If he's not gone before then, there will be only three in tomorrow night's picture.

Alice had my brothers again, which meant I belonged to her until I could find them. It also meant I'd be playing the part of her sword after all.

Chapter 17

I used one of the burners Jason Kim had given me to call Olivia's emergency phone, but she didn't answer. I got dressed in my red-wig disguise and tried calling again. And again. I called all the way to Willesden Green Station and again when I stood in front of the address that Alice had written along the bottom of the postcard she'd sent. I'd torn the card to bits and shoved it in the rubbish bin on the way out of my house so she could see what I thought of her threat if she looked. But I kept the photo with me.

Stan had rented a flat in a four-story building almost directly across from the Tube station, which made things both simple and difficult. Simple in that I wasn't forced to wander around a strange area for long, looking for the place. Difficult in that any fighting we did would easily alert the neighbors he had on all sides, bringing attention I couldn't afford.

I stopped in at the pharmacy before I approached his building, buying disposable gloves along with dish soap and sponges to make it look like I was going to be doing some cleaning. I started to head back toward his building, but something caught my eye as I passed the large window of a café, and I decided to go inside.

The café tables to my right were mostly full of customers, but the window was filled with computer desks, all of the monitors shaded to keep down the glare. The bright, shiny, red NEW painted across the window had caught my eye, and sitting just beneath it was Stan himself.

I kept my head down and found a seat on the café side, though the place was small enough to hear almost anything that was said. That included the tall, stocky waitress who bumped her hip against Stan's office chair as a "Hello."

"Didn't expect to see you here, Stan," she said, leaning down beside him to place his tea. "Weren't you the one going on about all the money you were coming into?"

Stan brightened. "And why would that keep me away?"

"I thought the first thing you'd do was buy yourself a computer for home."

"Maybe I did do that."

The waitress shoved out her bottom lip in a pretty little pout and shifted her serving tray to the other hand. "Then why come here?"

He leaned in closer to her and loud-whispered, "Can't muck up mine with all these porn sites, now can I?"

Stan winked, she giggled wickedly, and I rolled my eyes in disgust. I could think of much more pressing reasons to use a public computer. Though if his goal were to hide his identity, using the computer on the bottom floor of the building next door wasn't the cleverest trick.

When Stan finally got up from his cubicle, he grabbed a page off the printer and headed for the door of the café. I thought about following him up to his flat and getting on with my task, but his empty desk chair called to me. It was only a remote possibility, but if he did know where my brothers were heading, I had to know. If he didn't, I had to know that as well. So I scribbled a name on the sign-in sheet and sank down into Stan's still-warm chair to have a look.

When I was sure no one was watching, I opened a command window, ready to pull up the cache, but at the last minute thought better of it. Stan didn't strike me as much of a superspy, so I opened the browser history instead and found what I was looking for. He hadn't even bothered to cover his tracks. I suppose he decided that by the time anyone thought to look for his searches here, so many others would have used the computer it would push his sites well down the list.

That or he didn't care who saw. Because I was probably the only person in the world who would see a grown man's search of American boarding schools as sinister. A quick scan through the list of sites he'd visited showed that he hadn't been on the website of the school where my brothers were enrolled, but that only meant he hadn't looked it up in this latest search, of course. And more telling to me, anyway, was that he'd started his afternoon on a site called MoneyGram, which allowed anyone to send money the same day and had a pickup location at a jewelers not half a mile from the café.

Stan was my father's inside man, I was almost sure of it. He'd been the one on the other side of the phone call I'd overheard. I was less sure, however, that he'd killed Grady. Killing someone would only bring attention he wouldn't want if he was trying to get information to feed my dad, and the end result was to accelerate Alice's timeline, which gave him less time to get that information.

So, at worst, he'd spied on us all for my father, possibly shot at Alice, and Alice was using me to exact her revenge. But she didn't need to threaten me. I'd do what she asked, ending a life to keep my brothers safe. And then I'd end hers for the same reason. Because while I didn't want anyone to know where my brothers would be hiding in the States, I couldn't have Alice anywhere near them ever again. They needed to be away from all the death and threats and chaos. They needed a chance that I'd never have, to live a normal life.

And I'd give them that chance.

I was determined when I left the café. Ready. I thought about waiting in the area for Stan, to catch him outside and unaware, then end him in an alley to rot with the rest of the garbage. But it was too risky, and I still had to save my brothers from Alice. I couldn't be caught now—not this time.

So I stood outside the entrance of Stan's building, pretending to be searching my bag for a key. An older man took pity and let me in without any fuss. He only commented on how it was too warm out for me to be wearing such a bulky coat before getting onto the elevator. I climbed up the stairs to the third floor.

Outside Stan's door, I closed my eyes to take in all the sounds that I could. There was a TV on two doors down, loud and playing some kind of show with an audience. There was a distant baby's cry somewhere down the hall too, but the apartments on either side of me were so quiet they seemed vacant. And then I heard footsteps in Stan's flat and the sound of water running. He was home. I just had to get in.

In any city the size of London, where people are used to crime, no one ever wants to get involved. The idea that any-one would come to the aid of a damsel in distress becomes a myth when there are too many damsels and too much distress. Bystanders are notoriously deaf, dumb, and blind in the face of a scared or injured woman. If you're sick, bystanders are afraid to catch whatever you have. If you're in trouble, they look away, not wanting to entangle themselves in police state-ments or trials and not wanting to get hurt themselves.

But there is one exception. Everyone will stop and watch the drunk girl, because you never know when you'll get a good laugh. And I'd seen enough drunken behavior to emu-late it perfectly.

I stumbled into Stan's door and tried to get in using one of the keys I'd gotten from Lily Patel. It slid into the lock eas-ily enough, and when it wouldn't turn, I whimpered. I tried again and then a third time, jiggling the knob until Stan came up to his peephole to yell through the door.

"You've got the wrong flat!"

I lurched forward to press my cheek against the door, then opened my gloved hand to slap it against the metal. "Let me in, Stephen!" I slurred. "My key isn't working."

I glanced down the hall to make sure no one was going to

come out to see who was causing the ruckus, and no one did. They must have a couple of drunkards in this building.

"No Stephen here!" Stan shouted through the door. "Go away."

I stood upright, but made sure to keep my face down as I put my hands on my hips. "You let me in right now, Stephen." I wagged my finger and then swayed on my feet, only barely catching myself. "Right now, or I'll scream and keep screaming until the whole place knows how you mistreat me!"

I heard Stan curse and then click open the locks, which was when I slid my knife free and prepared myself. I'd have one shot at this. The very moment the door opened, I pushed in, trapping Stan up against the wall while the door swung shut behind me.

"What the bloody—?"

Those were his last words. I shoved my knife into his trachea, silencing him without all the spraying blood that occurred when I killed my father. I stood aside to pull it out and then watched as he held his hand to his throat and slid down the wall to sprawl on the ground. I was out of breath when I backed into the kitchen, and I couldn't seem to look away from Stan. He made a choking sound and blinked his eyes a lot, and it took him minutes and minutes to die, so long that I started to wonder if I shouldn't go over and put him out of his misery.

But in the end, his eyes stopped blinking and there were no more sounds. I knew I'd done it. I'd killed another man. My third. Just as many as Alice. A few short of my father's spree.

It had been so very easy to kill this man—too easy. A person shouldn't be that fragile. Adrenaline pumped through my whole body, but my mind was still. Was I supposed to justify this? Remind myself that he'd possibly killed Grady in the dark with no mercy? That he'd informed on us to my father? That if he wasn't dead, either Olivia or one of my brothers would be by tomorrow?

Were those things supposed to make me feel better?

Perhaps.

But I didn't feel particularly bad. I'd killed him and I just felt . . . normal. A little hyper. Quiet. Not even my thoughts plagued me, it was so quiet.

I dropped the knife into the sink, and the sound of it brought me back to a more practical state of mind. I used some of the liquid soap I'd purchased to wash the blood from it and my gloves. Then I used the shopping bag they'd given me at the pharmacy to hold my bloodstained trench coat. I left my wig and glasses on, and the gloves, until I made it outside the building and down the little alleyway to where the dumpsters were. They were all full, which was a good sign. Trash pickup was probably the next day. I shoved the bag with the trench coat deep into one dumpster and my glasses and gloves into another. Then I started back toward the gate, dumping my wig in a smaller can on the way and donning some sunglasses I'd stowed in my handbag.

I was still wiping the glove powder from between my fingers when I stepped out onto the street and came face-to-face with Sherlock Holmes. I watched his expression as it

rose and fell like a wave, from determination to confusion and
then to sorrow.

"I'm here to stop you," he said, though his heart wasn't in it.

"You're too late. And you're an idiot to be here."

I fed myself a mantra of truths, that I couldn't be responsible for Sherlock Holmes anymore. That he wasn't my business. That he could take care of himself. But I knew that he
was there because of me. I'd dared him to stop me, and there
he was. And if anyone saw him approach the building, he'd be
brought down on charges for sure.

"I've called the police."

"You haven't."

He waved me off, as though he wasn't just caught in a lie.
"I have to—"

"Go inside? Become a witness? What are you even doing
here?"

"What are *you* doing here, Mori? What have you done?"

His accusation should have made me angry, but my mind
was still so quiet, I couldn't even manage to feel that. I just felt
blank. "Go away, Lock. Nothing I do is any business of yours."

I started to walk away, but he made no move to follow
me. He stood still, wincing at the building like he was waiting for it to explode. Despite my dismissive words, I couldn't
let him go inside, I knew that much. So I grabbed a handful
of his coat and pulled him along with me, out of the main
thoroughfare and down into the doorway of the convenience
store next door. I let go of him by the rack of advertisements,
paced away, then turned to stalk back toward him.

"How are you here? How did you find me?"

Lock reached into his pocket and withdrew the wrinkled, taped-together postcard. He'd retrieved the pieces from my rubbish.

"Now explain why. Why are you following me around?"

"I told you I'd have to stop you."

"And how will you do that?"

He opened his mouth to speak, but I interrupted.

"No. Never mind. I don't want to know." I ripped the postcard from his hand, stormed away down the alley, and kept on toward the parallel street just ahead. But thanks to stupid Trent and his stupid training, I knew that Sherlock was following me. I had planned on taking the Tube back to my hotel to make sure I was at the airport by eight. I'd planned on hiding myself away to finish my business so that there would be no more postcards, no more taunting from Alice. But if I couldn't shake off Sherlock, she'd use him to find me, just like she'd done before.

So I veered away from the station entrance and into the café on the right. I knew he would follow me in eventually, so I went to the counter and ordered a teapot and two cups, then sat down at a table in the very back corner, away from the window, away from the chandelier that lit up the center of the shop.

Sure enough, Lock came in and sat across from me. He shrugged his coat off his shoulders, then stared at me expectantly, like he was waiting for answers. We sat in silence until well after the tea was delivered. I splashed some milk in the bottom of my cup and then placed a strainer and poured out the tea. I lifted the pot as a question, but Sherlock ignored me.

"Who is Stan?"

"No one for you to concern yourself with."

"But he's a concern of yours?"

I took a long sip of tea.

"What did you do to him?"

I should have said. Maybe, if I could have looked him full in the face and said the words, he would've been repulsed enough by me to walk away forever. Maybe that would have been the most merciful thing I could have done for Sherlock Holmes.

But he didn't need me to say it. Lock sounded in pain when he asked, "He would've hurt your brothers?"

"And he killed a man, if the postcard's to be believed. Does it matter? Does that make it all right?"

He couldn't answer that, but we both knew how he would. "Were those the only reasons? Who was he to you?"

"What do you want to hear, Lock? That he was about to kill all the children of London? That he was an abusive guard during my imprisonment? That he took the last Crunchie bar at Boots and earned my revenge? What would make you drop it and leave me be?"

Lock leaned back and studied my face for a second or two. "You were imprisoned?" Trust Sherlock to ferret out the one truth in the mess. "That whole time you were gone, you were locked away?"

I didn't answer. It didn't matter now that we were firmly

on opposite sides of his precious law. Nothing between us mattered.

"So you didn't choose to stay away? You didn't hide from me while I searched all of England for you? You were taken and imprisoned?"

I traced the lip of my teacup for a long minute before I spoke. "You almost found me." I looked up. "The place where I was kept, it was marked on your map."

Lock reached for my hand, but I pulled away. He frowned at the table for a few seconds, then asked, "What happened?"

"You were too late to save me. I was forced to save myself." I furrowed my brow to mask the emotions that were threatening to surface. "Turns out I'm not very good at it . . . the saving."

There was this long pause after I spoke—a substantial, spinning kind of silence that felt like a tornado of quiet had landed between us. But I couldn't tell if it was pushing us apart or pulling us toward its eye.

"Am I too late?" he asked.

He was so afraid when he asked that question. His voice was blank and cold, but I knew. And I was forced to look away, to hide my eyes.

"I have to go."

I stood, dropped a few notes onto the table, and tried to leave, but Lock held my hand. That was all it took to stop me. He didn't grab at me or even ask me to stay. He just reached out and took my hand.

"If I had been able to find you sooner—"

I closed my eyes, but it wasn't enough to escape his question, so I turned my head away, even though he was behind me already.

"If I had fought off your abusers and rescued you from your prison, could I have stopped—?"

"No." I said it quickly, to end his incessant talking. Every word he said felt like a weight on my chest, like my heart might stop if he said anything else. But it wasn't enough just to silence him. I needed him to never ask again. "Because I delight in it." I forced a smile into my voice, but I didn't trust my expression to ring true, so I kept my back to Sherlock as I spoke. "The look of fear on their faces when they see me makes my heart race. The power I feel as I give them the justice they deserve makes me feel more alive than anything I've done since that first day my drunken father swung his fist at Seanie and I stepped between them."

I turned my head to let him see my profile and said, "You were too late to save me the day you met me, Sherlock Holmes. I was never meant to be saved by you."

I slid my hand free, letting my fingertips linger against his before I took my first step away. It took all my resolve to keep my walk from the café steady and calm, but the moment I was outside, I ran to the Tube station. I had this imagined fantasy of me jumping onto a train before Lock could catch me, but I didn't even make it outside to the platform before he came up from behind and stopped me with his hand on my arm.

"I've said all I have to say to you."

When he held me still, I batted away his hand and turned

on him. "Does this make you happy? To treat me like I'm one of your mysteries? Are you on the case, detective?"

"What about you? Have you found your happiness?"

"Happiness." I almost laughed. "Do you think this makes me *happy*?"

"What's the word you used? Delight?"

"You think I get to be *happy*?! Can you not—"

"Why then? Why do all this if you get nothing from it?"

I struggled to take a breath, but the air only stuttered in and out. "For all your cleverness, you see nothing. You can spot the grass shards clinging to my feet, but nothing that matters. So tell me where I've been, Lock. Hm? Tell me where I'm going next. But never, ever try to tell me how I feel. You will never know. You see nothing."

"I see you—"

"Go away."

"I can't!"

I hadn't heard him yell in a while—not since our train ride back from Lewes, when he'd finally realized all the secrets I'd kept. If only he knew how many more there were now.

"I can't because I have to find a way to stop you."

He said "stop," but it sounded like "save" to my ears, and the cheek of that—that he would dare to think me another princess in a tower. I stepped up close to him and had to clench my jaw to keep my innate response in check. "Stop me from what? This world is a better place without those trash heaps in it. I'm cleaning house."

"That's not your job."

I moved back as naturally as I was able. I couldn't stay that close to him for long. "Whose job is it, then? The police? In case you forgot, those men *are* police."

"*Were* police."

I turned to look out the window just as the train whooshed up to the platform. I walked as quickly as I could for one of the doors. I couldn't be left there with him for another long interval. And if I hurried—

Lock grabbed my arm again when I was just about to board the train. "Please don't leave. Don't make me have to find you again."

I shook him off me and stepped onto the train before turning back to face him. "Don't bother. Just call *the police* next time. You do believe in them so."

The doors shut between us, and I grabbed the nearest pole to help hold me up. To hold me together. Tears streamed down my face as we sped through a tunnel, and I'd never been more grateful for the dark. Despite everything I'd done, that boy still affected me. And I couldn't let him. Not ever again.

Chapter 18

I reached Heathrow at 7:40 and stood under the purple-lit canopy of Terminal 3 just ten minutes later. And I waited. A bubble of panic started to form inside of me at eight o'clock, so that by quarter after, I was pacing and frantic. By half past, I had almost given up when I decided to make one more phone call.

"Mori, what's wrong?"

"Olivia?" I barely managed to say her name as the relief rushed out of me like an exhale. "Where are you?"

She paused. "In the place we are staying until the school year starts. The place we agreed on before?"

"Oh. Yes." My relief was cut short by the realization that I'd been played again. Olivia and the boys were fine. They never were in any danger. I kept telling myself that, but I couldn't settle my thoughts, because I had proof. I pulled the picture from my pocket and stared at it. Her scared face and not even Michael smiling behind her. "Did everything go all right in your travels?"

"Yes, of course."

"No run-ins with a stranger? Did you ever feel like you were being followed?"

"Not since we left England. Why?"

"What happened in England?"

"It was nothing, really. We were accosted by a teen girl who ran up and took pictures of us on the train. Claimed it was on a dare, but then she wouldn't give them over when I got angry. Gave me a scare at first, because I thought we'd been caught. But it was nothing in the end. And I didn't think it'd matter if anyone knew we'd once been on the Southern Line. Not now that we're out of the country and all. But really, it was nothing."

"Not nothing," I said, but before she could ask what I meant, I added, "I'm glad you're okay. I'm almost done with my business here. Shouldn't be too long."

"You sound tired. Are you taking care of yourself?"

Caretaking was evidently in Liv's blood. Another sign that I'd been right to trust her. "I'll rest when I'm done. Tell the boys I'm on my way?"

I could hear the smile in her voice when she said, "And that you miss them terribly?"

"Sure. That too." I ended the call.

It felt suddenly very cold standing under that canopy. Now that I knew my brothers really were thousands of miles away, I felt alone. Small. Like I might be swallowed up by the city, if I wasn't careful, and no one would ever know what had happened to me.

I had started back toward the Heathrow Tube station when

a man in a suit walked up in front of me carrying a sign with my name on it. I thought about walking by, ignoring what was sure to be more of Alice's game playing, but the mystery of it was too great. I had to know what it was all about.

"I'm Moriarty," I told the man.

He looked at the state of me and raised a brow. I could hardly blame him. I was wearing all black and carrying a giant sack of a handbag, my thick eye makeup was probably in ruins, and my hair had been under a wig for much of the day. But still he directed me to follow him.

"Where are we going?"

"To my car, miss."

"And where are you taking me in that car?"

"I've been instructed not to tell you."

It was perhaps the stupidest thing I could have done, but still I followed him to the car, only pausing when it was time to actually get inside. I thought about walking away again, but the idea of trekking back across the airport to the Tube station just seemed so exhausting.

"How much would it cost me to have you take me home?"

The driver seemed to think about that. "Where do you live?"

"Baker Street."

The driver's amusement should've been a clue, but I was just so very relieved when he nodded that I climbed into the back almost right away. It wasn't until we actually reached the house that everything came together. The light was on and the door was ajar. Someone was inside waiting for me.

"So, this is where you were instructed to take me?"

"Yes, miss. Sorry, miss."

"That's okay. I hope she pays you well."

"Yes. Very well."

The driver opened the door for me, but I didn't budge. I took a steadying breath and stared up at the ceiling. And then I stepped out onto the sidewalk. Again I was hit with the urge to run away. That made three times in just over an hour. I should probably have listened to my own instincts, but I didn't. In the end, I walked up my stoop and into my house to face whatever I'd find there.

It wasn't Alice.

That was all I could think as I pushed the door open farther to go inside. Alice would have been posed by the door, or would have left some kind of dramatic flourish waiting for me at the entrance. My first step into the house was silent. The house felt empty—or would have except for the sound of flipping papers coming from the kitchen.

I pulled the door shut behind me and slid the bolt to lock it, then grabbed for the umbrella kept by the door, but it wasn't there. I thought about searching for another weapon. I even indulged in images of my last fights in this entrance, of Mrs. Greeves dying on the floor because she believed a lie, of my own father tripping me up so I almost bashed my head against the door trim of the downstairs bedroom. Both times I'd been armed, but this time I shrugged it off and decided to trust my own abilities better than anything I could do with a stick.

I peered into the kitchen while I was still far enough away to run, but the shock over who sat at my kitchen table made me forget every need for caution. He was the last person I expected to see, doing the last thing I expected him to do.

"Detective Day," I said.

DS Day jumped in his seat and slammed my mum's scrapbook shut. He obviously wasn't the one who had hired the car to bring me home, which I supposed meant he was my postcard. Though I wasn't going to follow the message of this one. Did Alice honestly think I would kill this man in my own house?

"What are you doing here?" he asked.

"You first. How did you get in here?"

He looked from the book and up to me, then across the entry to what had once been my parents' room. "Was it you?"

I knew what he was asking. I knew he was there to find out about my father. I also knew he couldn't be trusted. "What are you doing in my house?"

"I have a key!" He pulled it out and slapped it down on the table like that somehow gave him the right to be there. It didn't.

"I trust you'll understand if I take that back."

He scowled at the key, and I thought for a moment he might snatch it up and hide it back in his pocket, but he didn't. "Where's your dad?"

"How would I know something like that?"

DS Day narrowed his eyes. "You wouldn't be here if you thought he was coming back."

"Wouldn't I? It's *my* house. And that is my book. What are you doing with it?"

"Did you make this?" he asked. He seemed almost relieved when I shook my head. I wanted to wipe that momentary reprieve from his face.

"No. My mum chronicled all the crimes you committed with my father, not me."

"What do you mean by crimes?" He pulled the book closer to him.

I walked farther into the kitchen to pull it out from beneath his hand. I sat across from him and opened the book. It naturally opened to the page about the Whitechapel street gang, only somehow the bottom of the article had come unglued from the page. When I flipped it up, there was writing underneath—my mum's simple script spelling out a name.

I looked from the writing up to DS Day. "Who is Barnaby Trenton?"

He tried his best to hide his reaction to the name, but his skin paled a bit, giving him away. "Criminal element."

"Who you all couldn't exploit?"

Day tried his best to sound indignant when he said, "We chased them out of the neighborhood! Those people should've been grateful."

"Grateful enough to pay you what they were paying the gang?"

He scowled and turned away. "Don't matter now. We've got the goods on him. Trent's not allowed back in London. That's the deal we made."

"Did you say 'Trent'?"

Day ignored me, but it was too late. I'd already put it together—the blackmail that Alice had on Trent. The reason my father had always hated Alice. Probably even the reason Trent had auditioned to become part of Sorte Juntos. He wanted to go back to London, but he couldn't if he wanted to stay out of prison. I wanted to know more, but the detective was back to asking about my dad.

"Tell me where your father is."

"Go and find him yourself. You're his friend. You're probably the only one who cares about his whereabouts."

"That's not true. He missed a bail check-in. They've sent us to find him. They're revoking his bail."

I stood up from the table, resting my hand on the scrapbook. "So, my dad goes back in prison where he belongs? Good."

DS Day rushed me and grabbed both my arms. "Tell me. Tell me what you've done to him."

I ripped myself free and shoved him back from me so hard, he fell down onto the bench seat of the kitchen table. "Don't you touch me," I ground out.

He flinched, and the look of fear on his face would have been delicious if I wasn't so angry.

"Get out of my house. And if I find you here again, I won't ask nicely."

He got up and eyed the key, but I stepped between him and the table, begging him to try it with my eyes. He didn't. Instead, he said, "Mallory will make the connection between your coming back to town and your dad's disappearance. You won't get away with it."

"I don't know what you're talking about. And I won't be here much longer."

Day rallied back, crossing his arms to stare me down. "I won't let you leave until I find out where he is, your dad."

I tilted my head and stared right into his eyes. "Are you sure you want to get in my way? That hasn't worked out so well for anyone else."

I'd probably said too much. And I couldn't seem to shed his threats even after he was gone. DS Day was dangerous for a lot of reasons, but I didn't need to bother with him. Not if he stayed out of my way.

That left me with only one more target before I could leave. I had to find Alice. Once she was gone, our lives could finally start over.

Chapter 19

I accidentally fell asleep at the house that night, and when I came out late the next morning, I instantly felt like someone was watching me. I walked up the street for a bit and stepped into a corner near a neighbor's front steps so I could scan up and down Baker Street. But everything seemed normal. I couldn't find anything amiss.

I wasn't even much bothered when a car pulled up outside my house, until a clearly rattled DS Day stepped out on the driver's side. He ran shaking hands over his thinning hair and straightened his jacket while he scanned the street, and then he walked up to my front door and started fiddling with the lock while still glancing around. He was breaking in. It was almost like he was begging me to end him.

I stayed hidden away at first, watching him, but when he got the door opened, I stepped out onto the sidewalk. I moved with purpose, not caring who saw. Let Day see me. Let him look in my eyes and know that he didn't have much longer to breathe.

A hand on my shoulder stopped me and I spun in place, glaring straight into the eyes of Mycroft Holmes.

"Come with me," he said.

I forced my expression into a more passive state, but I didn't answer his summons. Detective Day had already invaded my house, and I didn't have the time or interest to hear anything that Mycroft might say to me just then, even if it was about Sherlock—as it was bound to be. So when a group of chatty girls in school uniforms started walking toward us, I shrugged at him and turned to follow them back toward my house. I had no real hope that Mycroft would give up and leave me to my new direction. Still, I thought if I could just reach the house, maybe he'd wander off, or at the very least, refuse to make a scene in front of the girls.

And I was proved right for a few dozen steps. Or maybe it was that I had headed in the direction of 221, which made Mycroft think I was acquiescing to his request. Because the very minute I walked past his stoop, without even the slightest pause, he spoke up from behind me.

"One way or another, you and I will talk."

The confidence in his voice set me off and I stopped to calm myself, but gave in quickly after, turning on Mycroft and stepping close enough that our faces were but a few inches apart. "I have nothing to say to you. We are strangers now. Do not act like you recognize me on the street. I no longer recognize you."

His grin, which never seemed to falter, widened a bit, though his eyes grew cold. "Streetlight. Second floor of building 211. Rooftop of building 218."

I stared into his eyes for a few seconds and then turned

my head just enough to note that there was a man leaning his back against the street lamppost across the way, staring at his mobile. The rooftop of 218 Baker Street seemed unremarkable at first, but then I got the vaguest sense of movement near the west corner and saw a flash of something, like the sun reflecting off a lens. I didn't bother to look up at the second floor of 211. It was a better use of my time to attempt to control my breathing before I murdered Mycroft on the street with my bare hands while his government friends watched.

"Well, that's not a pleasant look," he said in an amiable tone that did nothing to lessen my rage.

"What do you want?"

"I haven't seen Sherlock in days. I want to know what you've done with him."

"I've nothing to do with him." The man across the street shifted his stance. "But what do you really want? I don't for a moment believe you'd have brought your goons out on a fishing expedition for your little brother."

"I want your first statement to be true." He reached a hand toward my head and I slapped it away. The man across the street reached inside his coat, but Mycroft waved him off. "Unfortunately, he has gotten into a bit of trouble that I assume is related to you."

"His troubles are his business and have nothing to do with me." I turned toward my house and started back along the walk, but I'd only taken a few steps when a man got out of a car parked on the street and adopted an at-ease military stance while looking right at me. I sighed.

"Sherlock was seen on a bus with a red substance smeared on his hands," Mycroft said.

I tried not to care, to cling to my rage and my purpose. I tried to tell myself that Lock deserved what he got, but Mycroft's words pierced through me because I knew it was my fault. I'd brought Sherlock to the nursery school as part of my ruse. I'd killed in front of him and left him there to struggle his way out. I'd done the one thing I'd feared most when it came to Lock. . . . I'd ruined him. I was very glad not to be facing Mycroft just then. "So? What does that have to do with me? It was probably one of his silly experiments gone wrong. He works with fake blood all the time."

"I thought as much. So when the report came in, I quashed it until I could confirm the story for myself. Which is when I found blood-spattered clothes in his room."

I closed my eyes. "An experiment, like I said."

"Human blood, as it turned out. Human blood that belongs to a disgraced detective sergeant who was released from jail a few short months ago to await his court date."

I composed my expression as best I could, then turned to face Mycroft, though I didn't say anything.

He didn't seem to mind my silence. "I hear they haven't been able to identify the burned corpse found in a derelict nursery school in Harrow."

"Really? Burned beyond recognition?"

"A superheating accelerant was used. It even melted the dental work away and shattered the teeth."

"And what has that to do with me?"

Mycroft paused, and for a few seconds I thought maybe his expression softened toward me. But the cold returned just in time for him to speak. "You will fix this."

"You said you quashed it."

Mycroft huffed out a soft laugh. "You play the villain so well, I sometimes forget how young and naive you are."

"Yes, and you in all your aged wisdom—"

Mycroft only took a step in my direction, but something about his bearing shifted so that even that slight movement interrupted my words. And then his expression became a smile that somehow appeared friendly but still felt like ice. "I am allowing you to fix your own mistake instead of taking you in, because I know you are the only person left to protect your brothers. I wasn't lying when I said I care for them."

He closed the gap between us with two more steps. I thought he might try to question me or study me—try to suss out the truth of all that had happened over these last few days and how Sherlock was involved. But instead he leaned in and spoke quietly at my ear. "I am allowing you this one indiscretion because of them and because of the brokenness I see in your eyes whenever I mention Sherlock."

I felt pain in my chest and closed my eyes against it. "Stop." I hadn't meant to plead with him, but even I could hear the plaintive tone in my voice.

Mycroft's voice was much softer when he said, "Make the case that he's your enemy, Mori. At least for show. It's the only way. The police have to believe he's been trying to stop you all along."

I released a shaky breath and opened my eyes. That wouldn't do. I could spend weeks setting an elaborate trail of evidence that Sherlock and I had been pitted in a battle of wits from the start, but Lock would undo all that work in a moment following his unending commitment to the truth and to the law. I'd need his cooperation to make something like that work, and Sherlock didn't seem to do anything just for show.

But I knew what I needed to do. I even knew how. It was the only way. My determination must have shown on my face, because Mycroft's expression shifted as well. I couldn't tell if he was concerned or amused. "So you'll do it?"

I nodded. "I'll make him hate me. I'll make him my enemy for real."

Mycroft didn't say another word. He turned to hide an expression I couldn't quite define, and then strolled off down the street in the opposite direction from his house and mine, like he'd always meant to go that way. Anyone looking might have thought he had a skip in his step, but I knew better. I didn't have to define his expression to recognize the sadness in it.

Chapter 20

By the time I got back to my house, DS Day was gone, but he'd managed to overturn all the boxes in my mum's room and rummage through the wardrobe. I wasn't too concerned until I realized the bed was shifted to the side, and then I realized what he'd come for. I'd hidden my mum's scrapbook between her mattress and box spring, and now it was gone.

It was a stupid thing to be angry over. I'd almost tossed the thing out myself. But it wasn't his. It was my mum's. That weak, nasty little man came into my house and stole from me. And when I went into the kitchen, I found that he'd left behind a note:

> *I can't let you have the book. He's gone now, and I get*
> *a second chance to start over. So I'm going to destroy the*
> *book and with it the person I became when I took orders*
> *from your dad. I'll smooth things over with Mallory if you*
> *just let me have this.*

"No," was my simple response to his letter. And then I started to move.

I was only going to his house to get my mum's book back, but I found myself putting on latex gloves and brown driving gloves on top of those. I spent the entire bus ride reliving all those times DS Day had stood on our doorstep, assuring us things would be fine and ignoring the cuts and bruises on my brothers' faces. How he would do this dumb little wave as he walked away, leaving us there with our abuser.

When I reached the stop on his street, my hands were squeezed into fists and I could only seem to think about the part he played in keeping my father in our lives even after he was in prison. How he'd called me with messages from my father, insisted that I go visit, even while I was still recovering in the hospital from what my father had done to me.

And then I was outside his house and I no longer cared about that bloody book. I just wanted DS Day to suffer at my hands.

I think he knew why I was there. He knew the moment he saw me, which was why it confused me when he opened the door to invite me in. I stepped in slowly, keeping Detective Day in my periphery for as long as I could. He moved carefully around me—always at a set distance and never making any quick moves.

It worked at first. There was even a second after I walked into his house that I felt sorry for the man. But then I realized he knew how to calm me because he'd spent so much time bowing and lowering his eyes in front of a monster. He played helper servant to my father so long, he'd learned how to handle his moods.

But that realization was also my undoing. The very idea that he would treat me the way he treated that murderer, that he thought I could be charmed into keeping him alive somehow! After all that he'd done.

He literally bowed a little to me when he said, "Come in. Have a seat."

And I couldn't take it anymore. "Do you think I'm here for tea?"

"No, but I—"

"Did you think I'd come over and we would chat about old times, like how you covered for my father when he was beating up my brothers?"

DS Day paled. "I have the book."

"Remember the time I called the police because I was afraid for our lives, and they sent YOU." He flinched as I advanced. "And you left us there with empty promises and a violent drunk."

"You can have it b-back," he said. But I didn't want that filthy thing back. I didn't want to see one more crime these *police* had committed in my city.

I moved toward him and he stepped back. "I stayed up that whole night, sitting on the stairs, holding a knife, and guarding my brothers so they could sleep because you couldn't be bothered to rescue us from that house!"

We moved like that—me advancing and him retreating— until his back was up against the counter.

"I didn't know it was that bad. I didn't!" He held his arms up, cowering from me. And all I could think was what a big strong policeman he was. How he had five inches on me and probably fifty pounds, but instead of standing his ground, instead of ordering me out of his house, he stood there shaking and whining, "I didn't know."

I had a knife in my pocket, but that seemed too easy a death for DS Day, my father's lackey number one. I wanted him to feel the pain my brothers felt. So I punched him as hard as I could, and he stumbled back against the edge of the counter before falling to his knees.

"You knew!" I said, my voice shaking with my rage. "You SAW the evidence of his violence on the faces of those poor boys." I slapped away his hands and punched him again. "You saw their eyes swollen shut and their split lips. You saw their blood and you did NOTHING!"

"I didn't know! I didn't know!"

He started to get up and I kicked him in the stomach.

"Well, now you'll know. You'll feel every single pain they ever felt. And then, maybe I'll do to you what you helped my father do to all those people in the park."

"Wait!" He held up his hands again and started to stand. I saw his hand reaching behind him and into a drawer even while he tried to distract me by holding my gaze. "I didn't do those things! I just passed on messages. That's all I ever did."

"Messages," I growled through clenched teeth. "Like the ones he wanted you to deliver to me?"

"To everybody. Just messages."

To everybody.

I stopped and Day released a breath and sagged against his kitchen counter. Not just to me. Of course not. Detective Day passed on messages from my father to everyone. Like to the officer who'd brought my dad's letter to Freddie's bed. He probably brought messages back, too, like the information my dad had on Alice living with us, and how he decided to fight for custody. And Parsons . . .

"Messages," I echoed. "Like a message to Officer Parsons?"

Day froze in place. He didn't even breathe.

"Was that you? Did you tell Parsons to go steal my brothers off the street?"

Day shook his head, but I knew the answer was yes.

"You told him to get a couple friends to help kidnap my brothers!"

"No!"

"And when they couldn't get the job done, when they scared my brother out into the street instead, was it *you* who told my father that his son was hit by a car? Is that the kind of message you mean?!"

"I had no choice!" Day shouted, pulling a large kitchen knife from behind his back and holding it out between us. "I'm a victim of your father too! He made me do it!"

"No." My lips twitched for a few seconds before I gave in to a smile. "You've never been the victim. But you're about to be."

I hadn't been allowed to train with knives in the barn with Trent, but we'd worked for hours on disarming opponents. Detective Day's knife trembled as he pointed it at me, so much that he might have dropped it himself in a few more seconds. I didn't wait.

I took a step toward him to get him to slash the knife in the space between us, and used his momentum to push his arm until the knife was pointed away from me. Then I grabbed his wrist and twisted until his grip loosened enough for me to bat the knife to the floor. He lunged after it, and I kneed him in the face. But he didn't stay down. He came at me again while I was kicking the blade away, and when I swung to punch him, Day blocked me and then slapped me across the face. I smiled through the strike, which I could tell unnerved him, but he pushed me away before I could land another blow. His next swing was so easily ducked, I almost laughed. But I used the force of it to turn him around and kicked him in the back to move him into the hall.

When he recovered, I punched him again, then again, and when he held his hands up to block his face, I punched him as hard as I could in his gut, making him fall to his knees once more. And I didn't stop. I kicked him once, then struck him over and over, long after he fell to the ground. My arms started to ache, and my hands felt like they were bruised and cut, even in my gloves. But I kept going until I was exhausted and kneeling next to him on the floor.

And when I did finally stop, Day moaned, "I'm sorry," through swollen lips and I just wanted to shake him until he knew that it was too late. But instead I pulled the knife from my pocket and opened it.

"Daddy?"

The voice came from behind me—a tiny, squeaky voice that sounded so much like Sean when he was younger. I spun into a crouch, my knife at the ready, but I didn't need it. The little boy in the hall wore pajamas with trucks on them. He started to cry at the sight of me, and he even looked like Seanie—only Seanie had liked dinosaurs more than trucks.

"Daddy?!"

He couldn't be there, that child. DS Day lived alone. He wasn't even married anymore. I didn't know he had a son. It wasn't possible.

"Please," the little boy said through his tears. "Please don't hurt Daddy!"

I was paralyzed by him. I knew what I needed to do—to finish off Day and get out of there—but I couldn't. I couldn't do something like that in front of this little boy who looked so much like my Seanie. He was so afraid.

"Am I dreaming?" I whispered.

The boy nodded, though he still cried. And he must have been right, because when I looked up, Sherlock was there.

Lock seemed to appear out of the shadows in the hall like he used to do when he was just pretend, though a part of me thought I had heard his footsteps on the linoleum. Still, he seemed like the obvious next part of this dream I was having, where Seanie was wearing the wrong pajamas and begging me not to kill the man responsible for his brother's wounds.

"Mori." My name on Lock's lips jolted me out of my state.

I watched him paint the scene with his gaze, take in every detail. He took a step toward the boy and then looked at me, confused.

"I didn't know he had a son," I said, as if somehow that should explain everything he'd just seen.

"And now you know." Sherlock's voice was different. It was like there was something caught in his throat and he was trying to speak around it. Like he was repulsed. By the state of DS Day? By me? He was staring at me, like I was supposed to tell him what to do next.

So I did.

"Stop me?" I didn't need to say "please." There were a hundred versions of the word in the sound of my voice.

And Lock heard them all. "You can stop yourself."

My vision blurred as tears gathered, and I let them fall down my bloody cheeks unchecked. "That's what you're here to do, right? You're here to stop me?"

"No. I'm here to help you stop. But you have to do it."

I shook my head too long, then stared at Day's broken and battered body. How long had he been unconscious? "You don't know what he did, what he knows. He has to die."

"The police are almost here. This isn't the way."

"You called the police again." I smiled, though I felt more tears well in my eyes. "Is that all you know how to do?"

"You can go before they get here. You can just leave."

I moved closer to Day's body and the little boy cried out. *He shouldn't see this part.* That was all I could think.

"Take the boy," I said, and lifted up my knife.

I could hear Lock's distress when he said, "Mori, let's all leave together."

"Take the boy or let him watch."

"Neither. We all leave together."

I dropped back down onto my knees next to DS Day, and I could hear his son's muffled weeping, but I couldn't let that shake me any longer. This man had left us to be terrorized over and over. He'd known the kind of monster my father was and had still played lackey to him like a beaten-down dog. And instead of standing up to him for once in his life, when my father had given the order to kidnap my brothers, DS Day had passed it along. He was as responsible for Michael's injuries as if he'd been driving the car that ran into him. And now he'd seen Lock there with me. He could not survive the night.

"Take him OUT!"

Both of them jumped, but then the room got quiet. So quiet I could hear the faint sounds of sirens in the distance.

"Ten seconds, Mori. You can give me that. I'll take the boy out and be back in ten seconds. You can even count them out."

I didn't even pause to consider. I said, "One. Two."

Lock rushed the boy out the front door and returned just as he said he would, in exactly ten seconds. But DS Day was dead before I got to five.

I dropped the knife on the floor and then stared at my gloved hands. They were covered in red, just like my mum's had been all those years ago when she'd been forced to kill her mark. It was just as my father had described. She'd needed a savior back then. At least mine wasn't a dirty cop.

I was sure Lock would keep me there and hand me over to the police. He did believe in their justice, my Lock. But instead he pulled me by my arm out a side door into the alley. When we came to the first dumpster around the corner, he carefully slid my bloody gloves off and buried them in the rotting muck. Then he covered me with his long woolen coat, grabbed my hand, and ran with me down the alley and out onto the street. The boy was nowhere in sight. We ran alongside a double-decker bus, jumped on when it stopped, and found seats in the very back corner.

He didn't say anything. Didn't let go of my hand. We just sat in silence through one stop and then another. And when the back area cleared out some, I couldn't stand the quiet anymore.

"Why didn't you hand me over?"

"I don't know."

"What are we doing now?"

"I don't know."

"Where are we going?"

"Home."

Chapter 21

When I was showered and changed, I came down the stairs to the front room. Lock sat on the edge of a wingback chair, like he'd been waiting for me the whole time. There was a tray with tea and Mrs. Hudson's sandwiches on the side table and a throw over the arm of the sofa. I didn't know what to do at first. It felt odd to be cared for, coddled like this. He was treating me like I was a victim of something when the opposite was true. But my exhaustion outweighed my confusion, and I gave in.

I curled up in the corner of the sofa and covered myself with the blanket, then held the tea mug between my hands to warm them. When I took my first sip, Sherlock stood. "My turn to wash up, then?"

"You're leaving me here?" I frowned at how pathetic that question sounded.

"Yes."

"Aren't you afraid I'll run off?"

His brow furrowed and his head tipped to the side a little when he said, "You could do that whether I'm here or not." And then he went upstairs.

I didn't wait long to follow him up. I'd spent so much time in his house, but never by myself. And the minute he left, his sitting room felt like a giant cavern—so quiet I could hear my own breathing. My thoughts echoed in that chamber, and they were filled with the voice of a little boy in truck pajamas calling for his daddy.

Four steps from the top of the stairs, I heard Lock's voice. I'd heard him speak like that just once before—to a name on a map. "I'm doing just what you asked."

When I didn't hear a reply, I curled up on the third stair and peeked up over the top and into his room. He stood by his bed, staring at his mobile, a pained look on his face. And without bringing his phone to his ear, he spoke again.

"You said yourself that this is the only way I know."

Slowly, I eased up another step so I could see better into his room. I followed his gaze from his phone to a pillow on his bed—the same one I'd attached my name to with a pushpin barely a week ago. Lock sat next to the pillow and put his hand on the paper, then looked back at his phone.

He nodded and then cursed. "Don't forgive me," he said, and then he closed his eyes, pressed his thumb to the screen of his mobile, and brought it to his ear.

He was going to do it. He was going to turn me in.

In a panic, I eased down two steps to make sure he wouldn't see me when I stood, then started downstairs for the door. The clanging of the postal slot stopped me for a few seconds—just long enough to allow the rational part of my brain to take over. I wasn't sure where I'd go. By the time he was done with his call, the police would have my name if not my physical body in custody. That meant it wouldn't be long before they cordoned off my house and posted alerts, possibly even to the evening news. I needed to get my stuff from the hotel.

At the bottom of the staircase, I stopped again. I also needed to take my dirty clothes with me, I knew, but when I reached the living room where they were, I ended up sitting again on the sofa and reaching for my tea with a shaky hand. I had to run. I still had Alice to deal with, and my brothers were waiting for me.

But I was so tired of running—tired of thinking and plotting and . . . and it was peaceful there in Lock's cavernous sitting room that had tea and sandwiches.

I stared out the front window at the people passing by on the street. There were an awful lot of them that day, and I knew why, though it took me a few minutes to put it together. It was sunny out for the first time in weeks of drizzling overcast. And it was a Sunday, which made the sunny day all that much more of a miracle.

It was a Sunday. And the post didn't come on Sundays.

I set my tea down with a crash that might have shattered a lesser-made mug, and I had the postcard in my hand before Lock could call down.

"Everything okay?"

"Yes, sorry. Misjudged my strength. Nothing's spilled."

There was this great pause that filled my head with racing thoughts of where and how quickly I could hide the postcard should he come down to check on me, but then I heard his bedroom door close, and I sank onto the nearest chair.

The *M* on this card was a series of four slashes. Alice hadn't even bothered to attempt a copy. And on the other side it simply read: *Bring my money to me.* There was an address scrawled underneath.

I grabbed my clothes and was gone before I could hear the faintest police siren.

My plan, when I left Sherlock's house, was to find the address but stay back and watch Alice from afar. I wasn't going to meet her. Not this time. Let her stew a bit. I was done being used by her.

But our meeting place wasn't some quiet out-of-the-way building, as I'd imagined. The address was for a family theme restaurant with a gift shop on the top floor. I had no choice but to go inside. Alice could have been anywhere in that tropical nightmare. I literally had to walk through a forest of exotic animal plushies and trees with faces to get to the restaurant entrance. And by the time I reached the stairs, the ceiling had turned into a kind of rain-forest fantasy, complete with giant butterflies, vines, and bright yellow flowers.

I walked down the stairs slowly, taking in the sounds of the place. But it was impossible to pick out anything real over the soundtrack of birdcalls and raucous splashes from all the water features and fish tanks. The very moment I reached the bottom, strobe lights started flashing in the trees, and the sounds of a thunderstorm took over for the birds. I frowned at a plaster elephant but stepped behind it to look around.

Alice was nowhere in sight, and moving through the tables

would only make me the more visible one. So I waved off the overly helpful hostess and headed for two giant toadstools, which acted like umbrella cover for a bar shaped like a snake. The bar top was even mosaic patterned to look like snakeskin, and there was some kind of cartoonish gecko creature peeking out at me from the side as I sat on a bar stool shaped like a tiger's back, complete with a braided rope tail. I couldn't hear much with a constant waterfall flowing behind me, but I was properly hidden in the darkest part of the room and able to see anyone who came in.

Sadly, none of that helped me in the end, as the person who'd come out to meet me was already in the restaurant. It took me much too long to see the figure attacking a plate of food just two stools down. In my defense, I was looking for a woman, not a man. I was looking for blond hair, not the vaguely militaristic buzz cut of Barnaby Trenton—the guard I once knew only as Trent. He had noticed me, however— either that or he found his food extremely amusing. Possible that it was both.

"They're called Lava Nachos," Trent said. He lifted his giant bowl of a wineglass. "And this is Survival Sangria. Clever."

He winked at me and I closed my eyes and sighed. But when I opened them again, I was staring straight at a bartender dressed in khakis and a polo shirt with a too-large safari helmet barely balancing on her head. "Would you like something from our juice bar, miss? Fresh lemonade? Our Amazon Energy drink will keep you up half the night to study but is so much healthier than coffee!"

I tried to wave her off, but Trent interjected, "She'll have that last one." He grinned at me. "Thinking about your health."

I didn't even wait for the bartender to walk away. "Still playing Alice's lackey? She couldn't bother to come herself?"

He seemed surprised at what I'd said. "Your plan was more effective than you intended. Alice is dead."

My mind was suddenly racing through how that changed everything I'd done in London up until now, but I didn't let myself react. He wasn't the only one with information. "Long live Barnaby Trenton?"

Trent's amusement evaporated. "Where did you hear that name?"

"Does it matter if I know who you are?"

He shrugged, and something about his indifference made me unreasonably angry. "What did Grady know?" That question got his attention. I didn't really care how or why Grady died, of course. He was just as bad as all the other cowards who thought it was okay to keep me locked in a cage. But seeing Trent's surprise made the question worth asking.

"How did you know it was me who killed him?"

"Stan was a plant from my father. He wanted information. He didn't need to play games with Alice or her men to get that information." I paused a moment. "And maybe Grady didn't know anything. You killed him just to make Alice scared so she'd up the timeline?"

My juice came in the time it took Trent to decide whether to answer me or not. In the end, he just said, "I want Alice's money."

"No."

I'd managed to surprise him again, though he tried to hide it. Trent had a shitty poker face. "I'm going to tell you a place, and you'll bring that cash to me if you don't want me to turn you in to the police for killing three men."

I shrugged. "Do as you will."

Trent narrowed his eyes. "I know where your brothers are."

"Liar."

He toyed with his food, then shoved it a little too hard away from him. The plate balanced precariously on the far edge of the bar top. "I'll ruin you."

"I'm already ruined. But if this is just about empty threats, I'll be going." I turned on my stool, but before I could stand, Trent grabbed my arm and spun me back around. I slapped him and he glared at me. I saw the bartender jump and start toward us in my periphery, but she backed off when I shook my head.

I watched Trent as I leaned slowly forward to sip my juice. "Don't look at me like that. I've been doing your bidding for days while you played the part of master criminal. But I'm done playing your games." I glanced up to meet his eyes. "I don't believe you anymore. And, if we're being honest, I haven't really believed you all along. It's just that your wishes and mine correlated."

"I've been following you. I have evidence—"

"I'm sure you do. I'm equally sure, Barnaby, that you're not about to walk into a police station and out yourself for being back in London."

I'd caught him there. His anger gave him away. "I'll call them anonymously."

I finished my juice and then nodded. "Do it."

I stood quickly this time and started for the stairs just as Trent grabbed my arm again. I slapped him off me and then yanked the front of his shirt to pull him close. "Don't touch me."

People were starting to stare, which made Trent visibly uncomfortable. He sneered down at me to cover his nervousness, but I didn't back down. Our growing audience would be my escape from him; he just didn't realize it yet.

"You think this is a game? Then here's my wild card: you're not afraid for yourself, fine. But I also have evidence on that boy who's been following you around. I could just as easily implicate him."

I swung my free hand up to slap him, but he blocked me. A server started toward us and Trent moved closer to me, negating the need for my hold on his shirt.

"Well, that got your attention. Maybe we should take this outside." Trent glanced around, grabbed my wrist, and tried to use it to yank me from the bar, but I was quicker and less afraid of causing a scene.

"I'm not going anywhere with you," I shouted in my most scared voice. "Stop threatening me!"

Two men and the server came to my rescue, surrounding Trent so I could leave, but he yelled after me, "Bring that money to Dover tomorrow at noon, or I'll take him down!"

I grabbed the first taxi I saw and took it to the hotel to

retrieve my bag, and then I decided to walk to the park. I needed to clear my head—needed to figure out what it was I even knew anymore. Everything had gone so topsy-turvy in the last hour, but now I knew a few things to be true:

Sherlock had informed on me to the police.

Alice was dead.

Trent was an ex-gangster who my dad ran out of town.

Trent used me to get rid of three of my father's men.

Trent was a threat to Sherlock.

Because of me.

That was the sticking point. I knew I could stay to deal with my Trent problem—knew too that if I didn't, he'd come for me eventually, that I'd never be free of him or my crimes. But if I stayed, Sherlock would be collateral damage. Trent would try to use Lock to get the money and keep me in line, but I never was very good at being told what to do. Eventually, I'd fight back, and win or lose, Sherlock would pay the price.

So I took my final journey down Baker Street, took in my final breaths of this city I loved, and made my way to the one place that would never again be my escape—Regent's Park. My nostalgia was cut short, however, by Sherlock Holmes, who stood at the very center of Clarence Bridge. He didn't say a word in greeting, didn't look at me, but when I walked past him, he fell into step next to me.

We walked together, passing the bandstand and Sadie's willow tree. We followed the main path past the amphitheater and then took a smaller one to find my fountain planter. But instead of retrieving my getaway stash, I found a nearby bench and sat.

Lock sat beside me without an invitation. He also spoke first.

"Is someone else dead?"

I glanced at him but didn't respond. And I shouldn't have looked. His profile in the dim lighting of the park brought back memories of other nights and other versions of me that felt so remote from who I'd become.

He nodded at my bags. "You're leaving."

I hated that he said it at all, but the *way* he said it—like he didn't think it was any big thing to me, to leave the only city that had ever been my home—tore at me. It felt like he'd stolen something dear to me, something I could never get back.

"Tomorrow?" he asked.

I tried to keep my voice as neutral as possible. "Tonight."

"Don't come back."

With only three words, he inflicted yet another pain on me that I wasn't allowed to show him. I hated him for that. He got to be the naive, entitled child pouting over his lost play friend, and I had to carry the weight of our loss on my shoulders and act as though I were light as a feather.

"You haven't given me much choice."

He jerked his head up to scrutinize my expression—still playing his little-boy games.

I said, "I know you called the police."

"You told me to stop you. How could I do that on my own?"

He looked so sincere when he asked, but I didn't answer him. We both knew he couldn't. Not by force, anyway. Maybe not at all.

"It's not like you would have stopped just because I asked."

My voice was much more calm than I felt inside when I said, "You never asked."

His brow furrowed. "That is why you left? Because I called the police?"

"No. I had somewhere to be. But you should call them again. Tell them you found me in the park."

I was grateful I couldn't make out his full expression in the dim lamppost light, because his voice was strained when he said, "If I do that, you'll . . . we'll . . ."

"Be enemies? We're already enemies."

"Are we?" he asked.

I felt a tear slip down my cheek.

He cleared his throat. "Just because we're on opposite sides of the law? Haven't we been that all along?"

I stared up at the moon. It was late and I had so long to travel before I could sleep again.

Sherlock answered his own question. "Maybe not. How would I know? I'm blind when it comes to you. I can't see reason or find my way through logic. That's the only explanation for it."

"For what?"

He looked down at his feet, and I did the same. There were bits of grass all around our shoes. "I still believe you can find who you were before and become that again. But I know you won't do it. Not unless you're caught."

"So in this little imagined world of yours where everyone gets a happy ending, mine starts with prison?"

"You have to face what you've done. You can't keep pretending it's right."

I stood and glared down at Lock. "Justice is what I've done. And I wouldn't have had to if your precious police force had an ounce of integrity."

"Not every—"

"Stop talking. I can't bear the sound of your voice."

He opened his mouth to speak again, but I walked over to the fountain before he could. No one was on the path just then, so I placed my whole hand on the Tree of Life and tipped it forward, then ran around to the other side to twist the lucky clover. I pulled all my belongings out of the chamber, including the envelope that held my mum's old fake identities. I didn't want to leave anything behind.

I paced away to shove everything into my bag, and when I looked back, Sherlock was toying with the fountain plaques like he'd found a new case to solve. "My final gift to him," I whispered. Then I turned and started walking away.

I barely made it ten steps when Lock called, "Not yet."

I clenched my fists at my sides, but I didn't slow down. I needed to catch the first train, which meant getting to Charing Cross Station as soon as possible. I didn't have time for him.

Not that it stopped him from coming up beside me. "Why does it have to be tonight?"

"Does it matter?" My quickest way was to catch a cab, which mostly meant completing the circular path around the gardens and crossing York Bridge to leave the park.

"Where will you go?"

I stopped. "Why ask when you know I won't answer?"

He started to reply, but I cut him off.

"Why are you here, Lock? I left you safe and in your house. Why did you end up in my way again? Why are you always in my way?!" When he didn't answer, I took a breath and started back down my path.

"The police are at my house," he said. "The boy has given his statement, and once I bring you in, they'll want mine as well."

"You aren't bringing me anywhere."

"You know I have to."

I stopped again but didn't turn around. "Will you call them now?"

"Do I need to?"

I stared at the ground, wondering how to answer him. I wouldn't be going back to his house with him, but would he believe me if I said I would? Would he try to force my hand? Did I have it in me to fight him—to truly fight, even if that meant beating him unconscious?

I decided not to say anything, and instead kept heading toward the entrance of the park. I did, however, pull my phone out of my pocket and type a text as I walked. Lock caught up to me, forcing me to put my phone away before I could be sure the text had sent. He kept a distance between us, though—like he was making himself walk farther away from me than he wanted. I shouldn't have cared or noticed, but I was grateful. It was getting harder to think clearly with him so close.

"Where will you go?" he asked again. "If not with me."

"Dover." I shouldn't have told him, even though it was only half the truth. "I'll take the ferry to France and then a plane to America." That was a lie, but he believed it. I needed him to because I couldn't let him follow me. But I did have to go to Dover to make sure Trent didn't follow me either.

"I'll go with you. Just to Dover."

"You can't."

"Then I'll chase you to Dover to bring you to justice." The way he said it—like he was suggesting we go to a café for a snack—made me hate him again. My struggles had always sounded trivial when he described them, my problems so easily solved by his version of justice. The world must be such a simple place when all can be parsed into rights and wrongs.

I shook my head and spotted a black cab parked on the other side of the bridge, almost like it was waiting for me. If I believed in luck like my mum had, I might have invited Lily to help me rob a bank that night. Then, at least, she'd get her heist. "Go home, Lock. Go back to your house and your police and tell them you saw me in the park."

He put his hand on my arm to stop me, and I shook him off. "Come with me."

I turned to face him, my mind desperately searching for that one thing I could say that would make him stop trying. I was saved from the task, however, by a man leaning against the nearest lamppost. And when I tried to focus on Lock instead of the man, I saw the flash of a lens just to the side of his head. That was how I knew my text had gone through, how I knew they were there—the government men. And I had never been more grateful for Mycroft Holmes.

Failed my mission, was the text I'd sent just minutes ago. *In the park now. Come and get him before the police find us together.*

But this was too fast, even for the mysterious Mycroft. I had to wonder if Sherlock knew he was being followed. Could they really have evaded his notice all this time?

"Tell your brother I said thanks." I nodded to the man leaning up against the streetlight to our left. The light blinked off just as I did, and the space around us went pitch black. In the next second, I heard a muffled shout from Sherlock, and then nothing. I felt an arm brush across my back, and I spun around, grabbing my assailant's wrist and twisting it up and back until I heard a grunt and something fell onto my shoe and bounced away. I didn't wait to let whoever it was recover. I leveraged the hold I had to push my attacker off balance and then ran for my cab. I couldn't afford to let them take me, too.

I dropped my phone and stomped on it just before I jumped into the backseat, dragging my bags in behind me. "Charing Cross Station, as quickly as you can."

The driver nodded and we were off before I could catch my breath. We'd barely driven two minutes when the driver looked at me in the rearview mirror and said, "You are Miss Moriarty?"

I wasn't sure whether to answer that or not, but the longer I took, the more obvious the answer was. So I finally said, "Yes."

The driver slipped me a white postcard through the divider. It had a slashed *M* on the back.

"Like it was waiting for me," I mumbled. "I suppose that means Lily's bank robbery is off."

"What was that, miss?"

I let my shoulders sag. "A man told you I'd be coming out of the park?"

"Yes, miss."

I sighed and looked at the front of the postcard.

> *Bring the money before the noon ferry, or your*
> *friend will be in jail before dinner.*

I stared at the address he'd written at the bottom for a few minutes, and then pulled out my last burner phone. I tapped in the number before I could talk myself out of it.

"Yes, hello. I would like to leave a message for Detective Inspector Mallory."

Chapter 22

The address Trent had given me was for a warehouse off
Jubilee Street in Dover. The place was abandoned that day, for
no reason I could discern, as it seemed to still be active and
full of bins and pulleys and carts, all with no one around to
push them. I'd gone straight to the warehouse the moment I
reached Dover, save a quick stop at an open-all-night shop for
some supplies. I had to be sure I'd get there first, and for good
reason. No one was supposed to see me there that day. I was
to be an observer only.

So I spent most of the morning hours looking for my hiding
spot. It took me a bit, but eventually I found a space high up on
a ledge that looked down on the warehouse floor. And when
I got up there, I found a little door, just big enough to push
a larger box through, that would give me a way to escape to
the outside without getting caught or stuck up there for a full
warehouse shift should the workers return. And then I waited.

Trent arrived at half past eleven and stood in the center
of the concrete floor, watching the main door. I had a weird
longing to climb down from my hiding spot and confront

him head-on, bare my teeth as it were. But I didn't, because I knew that was what he wanted, to posture and banter and possibly even toss me about and get in a few good punches before it was over. And because the minute I'd seen Trent's final postcard, I'd remembered something Alice once said to me: *Why actually do the deed when you can just move all the pieces into place and watch the game play out on its own?*

Yes. It was a lesson I needed, and it had taken me far too long to learn it. I was sure Alice had learned it from my mum, the master thief, who used a handful of crooks to take millions from ancient establishment coffers. Trent knew—he'd used me as his deadly queen to take out his opponents. And now I had moved the pieces into place that would take care of Trent on my behalf, and punish him for ever thinking he was a worthy opponent to me.

And I'd do it all while sitting up in my perch, hiding behind a group of boxes, and eating the tea and sandwiches I'd purchased at the store.

At exactly noon, I saw the panic on Trent's face as we both heard the screech of tires out front. And then the warehouse was flooded with flashing blue-and-white lights, followed by uniformed police. Mallory stormed in behind them, calling out orders and directing his men to seal off the room. Trent tried to run, but in the end he was pushed down to his knees in front of Mallory, his eyes wildly scanning through the endless crowd of officers for me.

"Where is she!?" Trent demanded.

But Mallory ignored him and started in with his police

caution, "Barnaby Trenton, you are under arrest for the murders of Officer William Parsons, retired Officer Stanley Gareth, and Detective Sergeant Geoffrey Day. You do not have to say anything, but it may harm your defense if you do not mention when questioned, something which you later rely on in court. . . ."

As I predicted, Trent was more outraged by my absence than he would ever have been by anything I could have said to him in person. And it was fun to watch. A moment of triumph, perhaps, after so many months of playing other people's games. I was having a bit too much fun, as it turned out, and I failed to notice the boy who entered the warehouse after Trent was dragged out. He, of course, noticed everything, my Lock. Even the fact that I was sitting up in a storage area among the boxes.

Our eyes met, and for that one second I wondered what would happen if I stayed where I was. Would he call out to his police friends to come and get me? Would he come up here himself? Would I have to hurt him to get away?

I couldn't take the chance. And I knew I didn't have much time, so I jumped up to use my escape before he figured out how to block it. I ducked through the cargo door and ran across the catwalk that connected this warehouse to another larger one next door. I sped across the roof and opened the hatch, then climbed down the ladder into an office, knowing I was ahead of Sherlock, but not by enough. So I took the extra minute to look around for a weapon of some kind—something I could use to subdue him without injuring him too badly.

I found a wide-brush shop broom outside the door of the office, and had the handle removed before he stepped foot in the warehouse. I briefly toyed with the idea of dropping my stick and making a run for it. Through the open warehouse doors on the far side, I could see the dock for the ferry that would take passengers from Dover to Calais, France. I knew the path I had to take to sneak through the fence and reach it in time. I also knew that Lock could easily catch up with me and there would be nothing I could do to keep him from chasing me to France.

Only I wasn't going to France, and he *had* to believe I was. They all needed to believe that. So I swung my stick around to get a feel for it while I waited for Lock to find me, then I turned to face him, trying very hard not to betray any of my emotions. I failed. I was sure of that. He jogged up, focused on the stick in my hand, obviously amused by it. But once he glanced up at my face, his amusement dropped away. Was he mirroring me? His expression was full of all the pain and loss and emptiness I felt.

Tears formed in my eyes and I looked away with a curse. I couldn't afford to give in to base sentimentality just then. I had to get out of there, follow my plan, and find my brothers. I'd promised them I'd be there. I couldn't let anyone stop me from keeping my promise—especially not Sherlock.

So I twirled the broom handle around my hand and focused on the fighting. I set my stance and pushed all the feelings aside, so when I looked back up at him, I could see only the opponent he was, not the boy I'd once cared for.

"Go away, Lock."

He'd come armed as well, with some kind of helper stick that had white-coated hooks on one end and a single nasty-looking metal hook on the other. Any hope I'd had to deal with him quickly vanished when I saw the determination in his eyes. "Not without you."

The ferry horn sounded and I checked over my shoulder to watch it pull into the dock. I was losing time.

"Let me take you to Mallory. We'll clear your name of the crimes you didn't do."

"And confess the ones I did?" I heard some yelling in the distance and peered around Lock out the other set of doors. A few uniformed officers were running in and out of spaces, like they were looking for something.

"Why are you here?"

"After the little stunt in the park, Mycroft told Mallory that I'd almost caught you there but you'd drugged me to keep me from following you. After I woke up, Mallory called me late last night to ask if I could come with him to Dover in the morning."

"Why in the world would he do that?"

"To find you."

"To find me," I echoed. "Because you know me better than he does."

Lock grinned. "Exactly. Only now we can go back together and tell him—"

"No. We can't." I grabbed the end of the stick and spun it behind my back to rest against my arm.

He held his stick in both hands like a sword, with the vinyl hook pointing out at me. "Just come with me so I don't have to hurt you," he said.

I bit back a smile, and he struck first. He swung the stick around and sliced it down through the air at me, but I easily fended off the blow, bringing up my arm and using my broomstick as a shield. He tried again and again to lunge at me with his weapon, but I deflected every attempt. I pivoted out of the way of his final blow and slapped the stick from his hands with mine. He tried to leap after it, but I brought the end of my broom handle under his chin and then jabbed him in the stomach once to push him away.

I kicked his weapon aside and leaned against mine as he recovered. "Are we done playing sword fight?"

The voices were getting louder. The officers were getting closer. And my heart sank as I realized what I was going to have to do to keep my word to Mycroft.

Lock still had his hands on his knees when he said, "Just listen to me—"

I grabbed him by his arms and righted him between me and the door the police would come through when they found us. They had to find Lock. I couldn't leave until I knew they would. "No, you listen. I'm not going to back to London. I don't want to." It was a pathetic lie, but I sold it as best I could.

Sherlock started to speak as I peered around him. I thought I heard an officer call his name, but no one was coming our way just yet.

"Don't talk. Just hear me. Trent has been the one pulling

my strings and sending me those postcards like the one you found. He's set this whole thing up and managed to capture evidence on both of us. You know what that means."

Of course he did. And the knowledge hardened his expression almost instantly. "This was all to keep him from following you?"

I saw a police officer peering into our warehouse, then talking into a radio. They'd found us at last. And that meant it was time. The thought of what I was about to do made me feel like I couldn't breathe right. "I needed a head start."

"And his evidence against me?"

"It won't matter. Because you've been trying to stop me all along."

Lock's eyes widened a bit as he took in what I was saying. He was so clever, my Lock. His voice was quiet and strained when he spoke his next words. "Don't pretend like you're doing this for me. I don't need or want your protection."

The ferry horn sounded again, and I glanced over my shoulder to watch the cars being directed onto the platform. I knew I was out of time, and still my hand shook when I dropped my grip on his arm and reached into the pocket of my coat. But before I could turn back to face Lock, I was in his arms.

"Please," he said into my ear. "Let me take you in. I'll fight with you at every step."

I couldn't breathe for a few seconds. Couldn't move. And then I felt myself curl into his embrace. It was all I could do to keep the whimper in my throat, keep the tears welling in my eyes from escaping down my cheeks. He couldn't know how good it felt to be surrounded by him, or how much it hurt to know it was the last time.

"I'll do anything," he said, holding me tighter. "Just don't run. Please."

I forced myself to break free of him, but I put a hand on his shoulder so that he'd look at me when I spoke. In the end I was the one who looked away. With my eyes averted from his, I said, "You're too late to save me."

And then I stabbed my knife into his side. He cried out and immediately fell forward against me. I bit back a cry of my own and held him up as best I could. He moved his hand toward the knife.

"Don't pull it out, whatever you do. I've tried to do as little damage as I could, but if you pull this out, you might bleed to death."

He stumbled back from me, and blood started dripping from his side to the floor.

"Stay still." I held out my arm and he took it, but he kept us far enough apart to stare into my eyes.

"Why?"

I let go of him, knowing he'd fall to the ground any second. "Do you not know?"

"When I see you again, we will be enemies." I heard the devastation that fed the monotone of his voice, saw his vacant expression.

"We were never meant to be anything else," I said. Would I spend the rest of my life trying to believe that lie?

He swayed on his feet. "You don't believe in fate."

"You don't have to believe in fate to see the inevitability of our destruction."

He didn't answer and I didn't walk away either, which created a pit of silence that threatened to pull us both in. Sherlock reached out to grasp my arm again.

"Let me go," I whispered.

"I could keep you here. I could stop you."

My eyes stung with fresh tears. "No one could ever keep me, Sherlock. No one ever will." I could have easily pulled myself free, but I waited until he released me, watched his hand tremble as it dropped to his side. And then I helped him down to the floor and stared out the door of the warehouse, smelled the sea air and my freedom. But the officers had disappeared from the warehouse doorway, and I couldn't leave until I knew the police would call for help.

I leaned down to whisper in Lock's ear. "Do you hate me?"

He didn't answer.

"Will you promise to hate me from now on?"

He opened his mouth to speak, though he'd grown too weak to say my name. And it was just as well, because Mallory had finally found us. I could see him and a few other officers through the side door, running toward us from the other warehouse, though they were too far away to catch me.

I ran to the open door, but turned my head just enough to see Lock one last time in my periphery. And then I sprinted for the ferry, which was already leaving. I pushed through the crowd of boarding passengers, only to refuse to get on at the very last second. Instead, I made my way along the shore.

I skirted the edge of the water until I was on the trail that would lead me to the car I had waiting. I didn't look back, not even for a moment. That was my gift to myself, my one respite from the shredding pain I felt inside. But I couldn't keep his name off my lips. As the driver pulled away toward the airport and my flight to Iceland, I vowed two things to myself. First, that I'd never return to the city I loved most. And second, that I'd never again love a boy the way I'd loved Sherlock Holmes.

Acknowledgments

Despite the many hours I spent all alone in my cave/office to make this book happen, I promise you it would not exist without the following people:

To Laurie McLean, my agent and friend. I adore you, and I look forward to partnering with you for all of what comes next. Thank you for everything!

To Catherine Laudone, who jumped in to help me finish this series strong and without taking shortcuts. Your encouraging words kept me going! Thanks to Ylva Erevall and Krista Vossen for my gorgeous covers and to Audrey Gibbons for spreading word of my books to the world. And special thanks to all the other S&S BFYR staff who believe in these books and continue to champion them.

To Kristin Crowley Held and Tracy Clark, who always put up with my chaotic thoughts and ugly drafts. And to Sophie Riggsby, who lets me go on and on about ideas and dreams and wishes, and basically inspires with SophieTime™ whenever we can manage it. I owe you all coffee, and probably dinner. Definitely cocktails after.

To all the bloggers and reviewers, librarians and booksellers who have supported and loved these books. You don't realize how much you keep me going with your notes and comments and excitement for what comes next. Thank you so much!

And finally, excess love to my family. Your constant support is everything. I love you more than Bob Ross loves happy little trees.